Descended

Amanda Lynn Almaraz

DESCENDED

Print ISBN: 978-1-7331714-0-3
Digital ISBN: 978-1-7331714-1-0

Cover Art by Eddie Molinar

Dedicated to my father, Anthony Almaraz for encouraging me to write; my older sibling Richard for always being available to help me edit; my super awesome friends Haley and Chantelle for listening to my insane stories for all the years I've known them; also my friends Eddie and Marcelino for putting up with my constant wishy-washy bullshit.

A special thanks to all the kids in the NEISD middle and high schools that I subbed for in 2018. You guys inspired Socorro and all of her fellow Heirs of the Round Table.

And last but not least, thanks Angle-fish. For being so overly enthusiastic about everything I have ever said. Love you, Librarian.

Thank you for your support.
I never thought I'd get this far.

Now… let's keep going!

CHAPTER ONE

A Child

Mondays have always been the worst. Any adult can tell you that a Monday is the worst. There's even a cartoon cat that my parents and grandparents used to read in the newspaper—back when newspapers were a thing—that said it was the worst. High school kids know it too. That's when we're suckered into giving up our little bit of freedom to be herded into a classroom, occasionally on threat of a fine for truancy. We stare dumbly at a smartboard, or a chalk board, or a dry erase board—whatever our disenfranchised school happens to have—and we pretend we're still comfortably sleeping at home in our beds.

I was failing my classes, everything but history, but I was still failing. I hadn't turned in assignments. Yes, I could read. I read remarkably well, and math wasn't too hard until they started substituting letters for numbers. I could do the work. The problem was I didn't want to, and at seventeen minutes away from eighteen years old—and only a few months from my supposed graduation day—the school had long ago given up. The counselors made a deal with my mom and told me I could turn in my work late for partial credit and still pass. I still didn't do it. What was the use? School didn't matter. It has always been about who you know and if your parents had money before you were born. I studied the American dream and found nothing but ashes.

In my mind, I was better off. I could always get a GED if I needed it and go to a trade school for the big bucks. Who needed thousands of dollars in student loans just to listen to people with a bunch of letters following their names talk at you for several months while you contemplate throwing yourself into oncoming traffic? At least, that's what social media had told me would happen.

No one could seem to comprehend how I paid attention in one class enough to pass with flying colors and ignore the others. Why couldn't I do that in every class? All or nothing! Yeah, my anxiety told me that too. That's why I did nothing.

"But you have a hundred in history!" my counselor complained.

"No thanks to Coach Old-Balls teaching it," I had told her. That earned me a stare. Apparently, calling teachers by off-the-wall descriptions of their genitalia got multiple parent-teacher conferences. That was the one time my father had managed to show up to one. He was not happy.

Mostly, I went to school for friends and for getting out of the house. I didn't cut classes. I learned what was on the board and lazily did work. If the paper was sent home with me, well then it made friends with the abyss. I don't know what the abyss was—desk, closet, backpack, life—but it was gone either way.

This Monday in particular, I stared at another slideshow from Coach Old-Balls on the Cold War. The desk was cold against the side of my face. This was my second time sitting through this dry, room temperature bologna of a lecture. Here I was again because, well, I failed the last time. Last time it was my after-lunch naptime class. Everyone had one, but I took it to gold medal levels.

Why they decided I needed to retake this class and not all of the others, or how I had even gotten to twelfth grade and wasn't still stuck in ninth, was beyond me. Either way, they fit the second semester of eleventh grade US History into my schedule.

This mind-numbing Monday, was also my birthday and I couldn't wait to get home, even if I didn't look like it. No student wanted to be in school for their birthday, it was ridiculous. One reason I didn't mind sitting in that class, however, was because the moment I got home I would have the unfortunate privilege of hearing my mother's wondrous tale of how she was in labor for twenty-eight hours without an epidural because she thought she was tough and could do without. She would then continue in far too much detail about how I waited until precisely two-fifteen in the afternoon to rocket out of her womb and scare the hell out of the doctor.

This seemed to be her favorite story. Everyone I ever met knew this story. My best friends Emily and Jake could recite the story word for word. We celebrated on Sunday this year just to skip the epic retelling of my birth. Jake still did a dramatic reenactment that would forever be scarred into my brain.

Today at two-fifteen in the afternoon, however, as I watched that minute hand click over to the three, I vomited. It came from nowhere. My body shook uncontrollably and I staggered as I rose to my feet. I shoved my way through the door of the classroom, falling over myself as I went. That sharp tang of bile sat at the back of my throat and saliva dripped from my mouth, snot from my nose. My feet acted as if they had never been a part of my body. My balance was a thing that had never existed.

Something was wrong, aside from what was wrong with me. I could feel the world around me shift, as if it weren't the planet that spun a thousand miles an hour on its axis as it tore through space. Instead, it felt like I was the only thing shooting through the galaxy. Everything spun, colors blurred together in a roaring whirlwind of fluorescent lighting, project posters, and neon after school club fliers.

Thankfully, I passed out. The last thing I remembered was the fluorescent lights high above me, the tubes blinding as they watched me from the ceiling. They had no sympathy for the sickly girl on the floor.

The office called my mom and she picked me up. What else could they do? For several minutes, I was entirely unconscious. They should have sent me to a hospital, but all they did was recommend I see a doctor. We didn't have insurance so my mom told them, "Yes, of course I will take her." She didn't.

We went home and she helped me into bed. I don't remember much even though I was conscious enough to know I was dazed and disoriented. Up was down and my equilibrium had taken a vacation. While it might have been a well deserved one for keeping me upright for most of eighteen years, it was still bad timing.

My mom took off my shoes and pulled my fleece blanket up to my chin. Vomit had miraculously missed my clothes, so my mom didn't bother undressing me. She placed a damp rag on my forehead and knelt at my bedside. I felt her hands on mine, gripping me tight in that uncertain time where my lungs struggled to take in the thick air around me. She closed her eyes and prayed.

My mother was an immigrant, and not the documented kind. She and my father had never married and while they were together, she was not a citizen. Sometimes she could find work. Usually, we relied on my father. I liked to think that he did what he could for us to get by. I had always hoped that was the case. The nagging feeling in the back of my mind said otherwise. He disappeared for days at a time and came home tired, sometimes with less money than he left with. We depended on him for food and shelter and when I looked at him, he never looked back at me. I was a window to look through, something that was never spoken of if it did its job. But if that window was dirty or broken?

My mother never questioned his departures, she was too busy trying to keep our meager belongings as tidy as possible. She preferred I stay home and play video games where she could watch me instead of getting dirty, ruining good clothes, or requiring more food than we were able to get. It left me skinny and ragged in my hand-patched clothes. In a world of flawless skin and great hair, I was the knobby-kneed kid in the random oversized hoodie—that no one remembered buying—and some cargo pants with far too many repairs. I was that kid that was usually avoided by the "cool" crowd, whoever *they* were... I rarely noticed people outside Emily, Jake, and Gabriella unless they pissed me off. Which, surprisingly, wasn't very many people. I treated others the way my father treated me. They were windows.

When I finally came to, I was still groggy. The world shifted around me as if I were a little silver ball on a tilting labyrinth game. I could feel the vibration of the late afternoon sun as it drifted into my room singing of dark blues with a waning chorus of orange. The moon, she was rising, the thinnest pale sliver in the sky. She was two days

5

away from a new moon and somehow I knew this.

As miraculous as the world felt around me—the rush of light making sound, and silence bursting with color—I felt absolutely disgusting.

Arguing echoed down the hall through my open door and I groaned. The last thing I wanted to hear was my parents going at it again when I wasn't sure if I was dying.

Sitting up was agony. The world swam, it was underwater, the posters on my wall undulated as if the house breathed like a sleeping beast. I got up too quickly and staggered from my bed. Catching the door frame, I leaned on it to steady myself. It didn't stop the hallway from tilting perilously. The hall closet was now the floor. It wasn't wide enough for me to walk through this way. If I was going forward, I would have to crawl.

My stomach roiled. I pushed off from the door frame and my socks slid across the ugly tile floor. How I managed to get to the bathroom, I wasn't sure, but I didn't want to vomit in my room. Everything was coming up, I could feel it fighting up through my throat with that sickeningly sour taste and I desperately put my hands over my mouth to try to stop it. As a note: hands do not stop vomit. In fact, it makes it go everywhere. Had I made it to the toilet, I imagined I might have felt some pride for not messing up the bathroom. Instead, I felt guilt. This watery stomach expulsion had gone everywhere and I didn't have the strength to avoid it. My legs gave out and I sank down to sit against the toilet. I clung to the bowl as another wave shot out from my guts. It looked like water. It felt like gel.

Sweat dripped down my forehead, down my neck. Snot dripped from my nostrils. My sweater was sweltering and the stench that came from it after the unfortunate puke-handed experience was nauseating. My chest ached from heaving. In between gasps, I tore my sweater over my head and whipped it away.

The cool air in the bathroom chilled the sweat on my skin. I shivered uncontrollably in the eerie silence that settled over me. The arguing had ceased in the other room and my heartbeat seemed to echo off the walls, counting the moments like a clock. Ticking the time away...

I swallowed hard and breathed out a shaking breath. It was entirely possible I hadn't heard one of my parents walk out. It happened often enough. Dad would disappear again, or mom would go sit in the car and cry. Half of their arguments didn't make sense anyway. They would start one minute shouting about finances and then next about something ridiculous like the knights in some fantasy book they were reading. I didn't understand it, and I didn't want to. Their verbal fights were terrible, but I had gotten used to that. The worst was when they stared at each other in silence as if their minds were at war through the space between them. I avoided them at times like that.

Tilting my head back, I found the blue ceiling of the bathroom was finally in focus. The light through the window was nearly nonexistent. Night had settled upon me while I sat cradling the toilet bowl for dear life. Whatever had made me sick felt as if it was finally passing. I could still taste the rancid stomach bile in my mouth.

Reaching up, I slapped the sink several times in the attempt to grab the rim. With a grunt, I pulled myself to my feet and my socks slid across the wet floor until I was unceremoniously dumped back to the off-white tile where I started.

My soggy socks followed the path of my disgraced hoodie.

I was already dancing in my own stomach-sauce, putting my bare feet in it wasn't much worse. I managed to stand with a death grip on the sink. The bathroom lights were still off. I hadn't managed to turn them on in my graceless descent to vomit-town.

The moment the lights flared to life above me, I winced and tried to look away. Movement in the mirror caught my attention and when I finally looked, I realized it was my reflection. I didn't look like myself. I was used to looking thin, but now I looked sickly. My dark hair clung to my skin from my cheeks to my shoulders. The bones along my collar stuck out. The shadow made by the harsh lighting only made the person in the mirror more grotesque. The straight scars on my shoulders were white, as if they wanted me to see them. They wanted to remind me why they were there and of all the ways I had failed.

Any other day, my skin was naturally tanned. Today, however, I looked gaunt and pale. I was a reanimated corpse. Leaning forward, I stared into my own hazel eyes. They were dilated in a way I had never seen before, including that one time at the eye doctor when I was little. The whites of my eyes were bloodshot, the tiny veins bloated or burst.

The longer I scrutinized myself in the mirror, the more things didn't seem right at all. I thought my eyes were hazel, the classic golden brown on the inside and gray-blue on the outside. Looking at myself in the mirror, they were only gray. That wasn't a real eye color, was it? I confess I didn't spend much time staring at myself in the mirror, I was never so vain, but I thought one thing I should have known was what color my own eyes were.

This gray-eyed stare was sharp, steely. My face was different. Was it even my own? Did it belong to someone else, or had I simply hit my head too hard at school? I was hoping for head trauma. Then, perhaps we could sue and money wouldn't be so tight. The day was certainly taking a much worse turn if I was hoping for a brain injury and a lawsuit.

The longer I stood staring at myself, the slimier I felt. I turned on the sink and cupped handfuls of water into my mouth. Try as I might, there was no getting rid of the aftertaste of whatever demon had come out of my innards. I splashed water on my face, and it didn't make a bit of difference. I felt slimier. I was a slug in human skin, though a slightly more refreshed slug.

The water dripped off of my skin and down my nose into the sink. I was reminded of the way my heartbeat had seemed to tick away the silent seconds. Those little droplets steadily *tap-tap-tapping* on the ceramic were rhythmic and slow. Time was passing and it unnerved me. Time was leaving me. Was I running out of it?

I heaved a sigh. The world around me felt steadier even if my own body felt much less so. I tried to remind myself it was only my anxiety getting the best of me. My anxiety, however, put up a fair argument that this wasn't its fault, but that I was some kind of terrible mess. It had a point.

Raising my gaze to the mirror once again, I leapt back. Before, I had looked strange in my own eyes. This time it wasn't my eyes at all that looked back at me. The face of an old man shown in the mirror and my mind thought somehow he was behind me. I snatched my toothbrush from its little sectioned holder and spun around prepared to fight with it. His laughter at my actions came from behind me and I spun back around ready to stab a false reflection.

The old man with his snow white hair and his long white

wizard beard smiled back at me. "There you are, Galahad," he said calmly and I glanced to either side of me.

My mirror was talking to me. This was head trauma.

"Who..?" I asked. And now I was talking back. This was some kind of psychosis.

"You!" he said with excitement. "We've been waiting for you."

"I'm dying," I lamented and sank to my knees.

"As if I have not heard that before," the man grumped. "When you are done being dramatic, Galahad, we are waiting for you in the other room."

"What?"

I looked up. The mirror was empty from my angle on the floor. Cautiously, I rose, slowly bringing my feet beneath me until all I saw were my own eyes peeking over the bottom of the mirror frame. I sighed in relief. He was gone.

Fever dreams. It had to be a fever dream. I touched my forehead and it was damp, cold, and clammy. No fever. Why wasn't there a fever? First, hopes of head trauma and psychosis, and then I was hoping for at least a little bit of a fever? I wanted something to make sense, for something to be wrong with me that explained all of this. Then again, this all could have been a very bad dream. I had a habit of lucid dreaming when my anxiety spiked, and boy-howdy had it spiked.

There was one thing in my favor: my feet decided to be feet again and steadied beneath me. Then it dawned on me. Budget-Gandalf in the mirror said they were waiting for me in the other room. My knees felt weak again and I thought I might drop once more. Who exactly was waiting?

Out of habit, I swiped the lever and flushed the toilet before edging out of the bathroom. The air felt lighter when I moved. With each step the eerie chill that had enveloped me in the bathroom quickly began to fade away. Our house didn't have central heat and air, and even in early spring the weather was already uncomfortably warm.

"Mom...?" I called nervously.

"In here," she said back. The words were short. Her voice was strained. Every time she sounded like that it meant my father was home. In truth, maybe neither of us actually liked him.

The hallway was dark. The sunlight from the kitchen had long faded, replaced by the harsh yellow-orange light from the fixtures in the dining room. My heart thumped against my ribcage so hard that my body trembled with each step I took. There was someone there with my mom, that much I knew and that put me on a fine edge I had never felt before. Did I need to run? Could I even escape from this stereotype wizard who could manifest in mirrors?

I stepped out of the hallway. At the rectangular table sat my mother. Across from her, as far from her as he could get, stood my father. Dad postured with his arms crossed, making a strong and almost threatening impression. There between them sat the man from the mirror. He looked the same: white hair, pale and wrinkled skin, and the brightest periwinkle eyes I had ever seen. I couldn't tell if he was smiling, I couldn't see his mouth for his long wispy beard. His eyes, though, sparkled with humor.

The tiny hairs all over my body stood on end when our eyes met. Instinct told me to run. Something else, however, told me I knew him. I planted my feet and squared my shoulders.

"Hello Galahad," the old man said to me.

I couldn't filter my language. "Who the fuck is Galahad?"

CHAPTER TWO

In Their Shadow

No one reprimanded me. While my mother never did, it was something that often set good ol' dad's fuse on fire. I typically settled for never speaking in his presence. Children were tolerated when seen and should never be heard. That seemed to be his ideology.

As for this old man, to his credit, he didn't say a word about my language. Usually, it was old people that bristled and then turned around and opened their mouth with a racist, bigoted tirade about kids these days.

Instead, the old man said, "Are you going to threaten me with your toothbrush again?"

I didn't realize it was still clenched in my right hand. I ran my thumb over it, feeling the ridges in the rubber of the handle. It grounded me, made me feel more in the moment with them. My heart began to steady and I breathed a little easier.

"Maybe," I said.

He chuckled his amusement at my plucky response and then changed the subject. "Time to pack, Galahad," he said.

"I will stab you with this toothbrush if you call me that one more time," I snapped. "And I'm not packing. I'm not going anywhere."

"Such violence," the old man sighed. He shook his head in dismay.

"It's this generation," my father said, "With their cell phones and video games, and all the garbage on television." My father was in his early forties, but with his fancy choice of words he could have been confused for some kind of elderly war veteran. He was a few classic lines away from shouting at children to get off of his lawn.

My mother glared at him. Her brown eyes that always looked at me with love and amusement—or the occasional bout of exasperation—looked back at my father with disappointment and anger. "Or perhaps it's because you never told her anything?" she spat at him, her accent becoming stronger now that she was growing angrier.

The rigidness in my father's stance evaporated and his arms hung limp at his side I could see the scar on his arm reaching down to his elbow, it peeked out from under his shirtsleeve. I had always been curious of it but I was never brave enough to ask.

"You didn't?" he whined to my mother.

"It's not *my* stupid family legacy," she said in her accented words. "And for the record, had I known, I would not have even considered having your child."

My blood ran cold in my veins. Was I a mistake? My stomach lurched again, but it wasn't the same feeling as before.

The old man shook his head. "For the record," he told them, "I did not approve of this match."

I felt sick.

"Shut up, Merlin," my mother snapped.

My father's face fell and he appeared immediately

apologetic. I had never seen something affect him. He had never appeared sorry for anything in my entire life.

A knife twisted in my heart and I didn't want to fall apart there in front of them. As all people my age know, the best thing to learn growing up: fake it 'til you make it. Yes, I was distraught, but I pushed a grin on my face and laughed, "Merlin? Like… that BBC show?"

"I hate television," the old man sighed heavily.

"Alright," I griped. "When ya'll wanna stop jerkin' me around, I'll be in my room." I turned my back on them to leave and my feet stuck to the ground, heavier than stone. My body moved against my will and I whipped back around to face the old man. Merlin, they had called him. I didn't know who he was, but I was beginning to understand that there were things he could do that normal people couldn't.

He held his hand out toward me as if beckoning me to take it from where he sat at the table. His hand rounded as if he had smoothed it across a sphere, curling it in his palm. He tapped the table with his fingertips. He wanted me to sit.

I grimaced, my jaw tight as the chair slid gently out from beneath the table. No one had touched it. No one had moved from where they were. And no one else seemed surprised!

"I'd rather stand," I growled through my teeth.

"You were never so troublesome," Merlin said to my father.

"I wasn't born at two-fifteen," he replied bitterly.

Two-fifteen? What did that mean? I rubbed my head. There was a headache forming. They were speaking in riddles and I had no context for what their relationship even was. I was waiting for this to turn into some horror movie where they spoke in tongues and I needed an old priest and a young priest or those guys from that show with the 1967 Chevy

Impala.

When it appeared as if the two men weren't going to say much more, my mother leveled her gaze on me and said, "Go pack your things, *mija*. Things you'll need for a week or two."

"One bag, preferably," Merlin added.

"Better pitch for the baggage fee, old man," I said and headed for my room.

Behind me I heard, "What is a baggage fee?"

"Airplanes, Merlin," my father said. "Airplanes."

Shirts, pants, shorts, underwear, bras, socks, deodorant—couldn't forget that—hairbrush, I ticked the things off as I went over them. Cell phone, wall charger. I'd hate to be without those. I was a little upset that I only filled one small duffel bag, but those were the immediate things and I had survived on less.

When I returned from my room, Merlin stood by the couch with my father. My mother still sat at the table, her hands clasped together and her eyes closed. She whispered into her hands a prayer that I couldn't hear. I knew it was for me, though. There was always a way about her when she prayed for me. She meant it more than anything. She had faith in her words that were only for God.

"Mom?" I asked. I noticed no one else had a bag except me. "You're coming, right?"

She lowered her hands when I spoke to her and she smoothed them over the yellow table cloth. "Not yet," she said and gave me a weak smile.

"Not yet?" I repeated slowly.

"She'll join us when everything is ready to be moved," my father said.

I looked directly back at him, stared at him. He was lying.

I dropped my bag at my feet and said, "I don't trust you."

A strangled sob raised from my mother. I didn't want to look back. I didn't want to take my gaze off of my father. He wasn't to be trusted. A knot formed in my stomach, a lump in my throat. My mom wasn't coming with us and no one wanted to tell me. They would rather lie and pretend it was easier. It wasn't easier on me. It was never easier on me.

"Erik," Merlin softly reprimanded my father, "you shouldn't have lied."

"She wouldn't have noticed," my father said.

That frozen dagger lanced through my heart once again and my veins flooded with ice. I trembled. How could he think such a thing? I wasn't oblivious to the world around me.

This is something all people my age desperately wish their parents were able to understand. We are not mindless and constantly distracted. We are hyper-aware of the state of the world. Through the entirety of high school we are told to choose the direction for the rest of our lives when we're teenagers. We're told we have to behave and act like adults if we want to be treated like one, and even if we bend over backward with our responsibilities and somehow come out on top, we are constantly belittled with statements that we are too young to know how the world works. They say we are too young to make adult choices. I was tired of this. I was tired of all of this, of everyone making decisions for my benefit without asking me how I truly felt.

"Wouldn't have noticed?" I shouted.

"Galahad," Merlin said and my attention reluctantly left my father.

That name wasn't mine, though that same feeling inside me that told me I knew Merlin said that this was not a bad thing to be called. It was becoming a familiar feeling. I didn't want it to be.

"Only the blood of the knights may come with us."

"Make an exception," I snapped.

"I cannot," Merlin told me. "We do not have the resources to take all of the families. And it is not forever. You are allowed to visit your mother whenever you wish. I will show you how when we get there."

My gut told me to trust him, that he was telling the truth. As confident that I was that my father had initially lied, I was equally confident that Merlin told the truth. "Promise?" I said softly.

"Of course, Gala—" he paused and his fluffy white brows furrowed. "What is your name?"

"Socorro," I said proudly. My father's expression slid from proud to deeply annoyed.

"Helpful," Merlin mused. "Fitting, though not expected."

"Her name is Ilar," my father cut in.

Blandly, Merlin said, "Hilarious. She is anything but."

They were speaking in tongues again. I knew the words they spoke, but there was an unmentioned context that I just didn't get.

"We can't all be Welsh," Merlin clucked. "I've met so many Llewelyns I can hardly keep them straight."

Merlin's words made absolutely no sense to me.

The strap of my bag came over my shoulder. My mother stood at my side. She smiled with tears caught in her dark eyelashes. She kissed my forehead and froze. Her hands held either side of my face and she held my gaze. Worry creased her brow. "What's wrong with your eyes?" she asked and turned my head right and left as she examined me.

"Head trauma?" I suggested.

"Her body is getting used to the magic in the world," Merlin said offhandedly.

I laughed, "Yeah. O-kay."

"None of the others had any issues with vomiting or passing out though," Merlin said. "It is probably because you are so small."

I stared at him. Small, he had said. Thin, he meant. And there were others? What kind of others? What were we? Merlin had said something about blood of knights and the more I thought about it, the more it was feeling a bit like a cult. Had I been born into a cult?

My headache was quickly worsening.

"Oh!" Merlin said, he had turned to walk away and then swung back with all of his attention on me. I took a half-step back as if catching the weight of a physical blow. "Your toothbrush."

"My toothbrush?" I asked.

"You did not pack it," he told me

I went over my things in my head once more and realized I had left it on my bed. "Oh…" I muttered and dropped my bag to retrieve it.

When I returned, my father was gone. My mother sat at the table again. Merlin remained unmoved from where I had left him. He was waiting for me. "Before we go," he said. "What is this all over you?"

I looked down at my clothes and the white residue that stained the fabric and left dusty marks on my skin. "Ha… uh… Puke?" I replied.

"You're disgusting," he told me.

"You're not exactly giving me the time for a shower," I shot back.

"Are you going barefoot as well?"

"They're the only thing not covered in all the chuck of the up kind." I patted my bag as I lifted it to my shoulder again. I'd packed my shoes away for a cleaner day.

The old man glared at me. A wordless grumble came from deep in his throat and he raised his hand and snapped his fingers.

The air felt odd around me. That white residue was gone. My clothes even smelled like they were fresh out of the dryer. I wished I felt as if I were fresh out of the dryer. There was a film on my skin, I could feel it even though I felt clean. It was irritating.

"Happy now?" I asked.

"A little," he replied shortly and then motioned to my bare feet. "Now put your shoes on."

I mocked his words with a shake of my head as I did as he ordered.

The moment I stood up straight, he said, "Come now."

"You promised," I reminded him with a point of my finger.

"I did," he said and beckoned me forward. I looked to my mother for some kind of indication that it was safe to go and she smiled so weakly that I had to look away. She didn't want me to go. I didn't want to go. I was as accommodating as possible, but I was dragging my feet.

It was best I go, wasn't it? They all wanted me to go and I had a feeling that if I tried to stay, Merlin wouldn't let me. He had stopped me before and he had some command of… something unnatural. Magic was the implication. Real magic. I didn't know how to feel about that.

I followed him as he walked to the laundry room and I blinked slowly at faded green paint on the door. Once upon a time it had been an outside laundry room. Winter one year was cold enough that it was finally enclosed as part of the living room. There was nothing fantastical about that door. It only led to the washer and dryer.

"Yup…" I muttered. "Whole family is nuts…"

"So quick to doubt," he said and gave a wave of his hand. He opened the door and it certainly was not the washer and dryer I was used to seeing. Through the doorway was a rounded set of white, stone arches that extended to the right and left. Through the arches were trees, thick green trees that I could see no end to. The concrete slab where I often dropped my socks had become wavy gray stone bricks and blocks.

"Hurry, I do not have all day," he chastised.

My house was stuffy and warm. I passed through that doorway into cool, crisp air and shivered. I hugged myself. My hoodie was still soiled in the bathroom. Of course I had another, but it was packed away. Merlin stepped up beside me and I glanced the direction we came. There was nothing behind me but the arches. We were surrounded by them, encircled. I took a few short steps forward and turned around to take it in. At my back was fire inset in the middle of that gray flagstone foundation. A meeting place? A place for rituals?

"What are you, a wizard?" I asked. I was trying desperately not to panic.

He stared at me. For a really long time he stared with this annoyed disbelief. Had no one ever asked him that before?

When it seemed he wouldn't answer, I said, "Alright. You said you would show me how to go back. Now show me." I needed to know I could go home, that I wasn't trapped here.

"I did promise," he sighed. "But you cannot stay long, there are things that need to be done here."

"Show me," I ordered.

Once more, the old man stared at me. "Attitude, attitude," he muttered. "That needs to be fixed."

I dropped my bag with a thud and crossed my arms.

"Touch the stone," he said.

Annoyed with his words, I stared at him and slapped my hand onto the white stone of a column. It was rough under my skin. It looked like it should have been smooth. The stone was unfinished and the longer I looked at it, I could see tool marks: scoring chisel chips along the corners to blunt the edges.

Merlin took a deep breath and held it. Was he counting to ten? Exhaling, he said, "Now think of where you wish to go."

Staring at the stone, I could see nothing but its craggy surface. I had to close my eyes and see the living room. I imagined myself walking through the front door of my house, the way I did so many times after school. The awful tile flooring showed its many colors. It was ugly, but in my mind it brought comfort. To my left was that old worn couch, and straight ahead the dining table where I had left my mother sitting only brief moments ago.

"Now walk through," Merlin said.

I opened my eyes and I was looking into my home, into the living room from the front door. I ran through it. The dining room light was still on, but my mother was no longer at the table. "Mom?" I called out.

My brain was running away from me. There was some fear of object permanence in my head. I had gone to a different world. If I left her, had she entirely ceased to exist? Was she gone now? Was there no one left in the house? Merlin said I could come back, he didn't say she would be here when I did. I felt queasy.

My mother peeked around the corner from the kitchen and

I ran into her arms. At first, I thought it was only her crying. It was me, too. I sobbed against her and clutched her shirt like a toddler. I thought that I was perfectly fine on my own, without either of them. I didn't know I would feel this way, this heartbroken that she couldn't come with me. Who was going to pray for me when I got hurt, or pretend to threaten me with a chancla for guessing how a movie would end less than halfway through. I didn't hate her. How could I?

"Trust Merlin, *mija*," she said and kissed the top of my head. "He will take care of you."

"I'll see you again, right?" I asked through a snotty sniffle.

"Of course, of course," she assured me and held me tighter. She would continue to exist here. Alive, but separate from me. My chest ached. I hated this.

She reached out to the chair she had been sitting in when I left and held out my hoodie. "You can't forget this," she said and pulled it over my head. It was clean and smelled of the last time I washed it. Had Merlin's magic cleaned it too? Or did time work differently in that other place and she had done a load of laundry in the few moments I had been gone? I didn't want to think too much on it. Anything seemed possible.

I pushed my hands out through the sleeves and hugged her again.

"Now go on," she said and this time when she smiled, her heart was in it. "Go. It's like a new day of a really weird school. Go."

"That's a little disheartening," I muttered.

"Oh," she clucked. "That's a lot of syllables for someone failing English."

"Ouch..." My mother was savage. She turned me back toward the front door and I saw Merlin waiting for me.

Could she see him standing there, too? Or was she kicking me out the front door?

Reluctantly, I crossed the threshold, hesitating for a moment with my left foot hovering in the air. I felt the portal close behind me. Everything normal in my life was cut off. The columns loomed around me and I felt an unusual sense of peace wash over my body. I didn't like it. It was disarming and it put me more on edge than I was prepared for. My lungs hurt, my nostrils flared. The air was different, sweeter. What was I doing in this place? I didn't belong here.

"Socorro?" Merlin addressed me and my attention snapped to him as if he had cracked a whip. "Breathe, and wipe your nose," he said calmly. "By god, girl, you are the most worked up descendant I have met."

What was a descendant? I knew the original meaning of the word, but the way he said it was odd. It was a title. Descendant. Of knight's blood? What knights?

I wiped the back of my arm across my nose and left a streak of dried snot across my newly cleaned hoodie. Merlin looked at me with a frown of disgust.

With an absent wave of his hand, my bag lifted back onto my shoulder and I sagged with an *oomph* when the weight dropped. He gestured for me to follow him. Once more, I hesitated.

Halfway across the circle from me he said over his shoulder, "You shouldn't keep them waiting."

"Keep who waiting?" I called back.

"Everyone," he said and continued on. "You're the last descendant to arrive."

"What? Descendant of what?" I called back. "Merlin! Descendant of what?"

Merlin was not a friend to my anxiety.

So far I had been getting my way by yelling at him. That did not seem to be the case at this moment. Merlin kept walking straight through the arches where he left that gray stone circle and descended the grassy ledge. I ran. I didn't want to be left behind, not in this strange place.

The moment I hit the end of the circle, I froze, teetering on the top of a set of stairs. Cheering filled the air and I staggered back in fright. People. Hundreds of people clapped and threw their hands in the air. No, they were throwing flowers. Flowers rained like confetti before me, thrown by people I didn't know.

I thought my heart would fail me. I didn't have the constitution for large crowds and large commotions. This would be the death of me. Merlin would be the death of me.

"Come now," Merlin said and waved me forward. I barely heard him.

I took one tentative step and my body refused to go any further. I couldn't do it. I couldn't willingly step down into this mass of strangers. I didn't care how excited they were, I wanted to run. The quiet of my bedroom was safe. This place with its trees and its midday sunshine was beyond dangerous. My hands trembled at my sides and I gripped the strap of my bag. No, there was no way I was willingly descending into this madness!

Spinning around, I barely lifted my right foot before the weight of moving was too much. I slung forward and hit the ground with all the force of my own body. This was not me being clumsy. I was not that terrible at walking.

The cheering was over with a resounding "Oooooh". I could almost hear them wincing. I had hit the ground hard. They had certainly heard it.

"Alright, alright," I heard. English accent, male. He cast his voice over the murmurs. "Let's give her some space."

Rising to my knees, I rubbed at my cheek. Luckily, I'd had the sense to turn my head and not take the impact against the stone straight to my chin. That might have been disastrous.

"Do not make me do that again," I heard Merlin say and turned on my knees to look back at him. He had come to the top of the stairs to reprimand me. "You are making this much harder on yourself."

"Harder on myself?" I shot back. "No one told me what's going on, just that I should trust you and you keep—"

"I am keeping you from running away, like a coward," Merlin told me.

I was bristling. Sure, I didn't think I was a box of bravery, but a coward? No one had ever called me that, at least not where I could hear them. I shoved myself to my feet and snatched up my bag once more. "Go fuck yourself Merlin."

"Whoa!" came that voice again, the one that had sent away the crowd. "Easy there Galahad," he said from halfway up the stairs.

Dark skin and brown eyes, he was much taller than me and I could tell that even when I was looking down at him. He had a pleasant face, one that said he was used to peacekeeping. He looked like a peacekeeper, a mediator.

"Next person that calls me Galahad, I'll—"

"What?" Merlin interrupted with a grump. "Stab them with your toothbrush?"

"Alright..." said the young man. Young, he was my age, maybe a little older. "Ilar—"

"Socorro!" I sharply corrected him.

He took it in stride. "Socorro," he said and gave me a smile. "Your father told us you were on your way. He introduced you by your other name, so I apologize if we call you that for a bit. Please be patient with us while we get to know you."

I cast Merlin a glance. "Is this guy for real?" I scoffed.

Merlin sighed. "Socorro, this is Henry. Henry is the heir of King Arthur and Queen Guinevere."

I looked between them and rudely chuckled, "That means absolutely nothing to me."

Henry was crestfallen for a very short moment, and then an amused smile crossed his lips.

Merlin said, "Who is Arthur in that television show you watched?"

"I didn't say I watched it. I just read the summary, and looked at the hot guys in the previews," I grumbled.

Merlin took a deep breath. He was steadying himself again. I could see him counting to ten this time and I counted with him. He released it in a huff when I reached ten. I was right.

Henry said, "That's fine. I'm sure one of us can catch you up on the culture here. Just like going to school."

"I'll pass," I said, holding up my hand to stop that thought right there.

Henry stared at me. He blinked once. Twice. I imagined he was counting to ten as well. "May I show you around?" he asked and before I could object, he added, "I can show you where you'll be staying. I'm sure your bag is cumbersome."

"Cumbersome means—" Merlin began.

I cut him off with an exasperated, "I know what cumbersome means!"

"Could have fooled me," the old man said.

And then for good measure I joked, "It's the last name of that actor, right? Bandersnatch Cumbersome?"

"You are the worst," I thought I heard Merlin grumble as he began to descend the stairs. I bit back a smirk. I was getting under his skin. Good. He hadn't exactly been very nice. "I leave you in Henry's capable hands," he told me and simply walked away.

My smile was gone. If I tried to run again, I knew I'd end up on the ground. After steeling myself to the coming stress of being forced to meet new people and actually talk to them, I started down towards Henry. When I stood a few steps above him, I said, "Keep your capable hands to yourself."

He raised his hands in surrender and then made a show of securely stowing them in his pockets. I looked him over as we stood there. He was normal enough in jeans and a well fitting t-shirt with some brand or band I had never heard of scrawled across the front in white letters.

As I looked around, the people I saw milling about were dressed like nothing out of the ordinary, casual. They didn't look like they belonged on the other side of a magic portal.

Merlin was the strange one with his wizard beard, walking around in an old red robe like some extra from The Hobbit.

Henry trotted down the stairs and I followed with much less enthusiasm. I didn't follow at his side, but to his credit he kept an easy pace as we walked beneath the much-too-green trees. People waved to him. He waved back. They muttered to one another when I didn't wave at all. Again, to Henry's credit, he didn't force me to talk.

Not wanting to feel their attention, I reached back and pulled the hood of my black sweater over my head. It was like blinders on a horse. Those people ceased to exist and I felt better.

The treeline finally broke to reveal a sprawling village with low-laying thatched roofs and a great serene lake. Smoke came from a few of the chimneys of the buildings and I groaned. Anyone I knew would have checked long before, but I was a bit late to the realization. Seeing those houses with their simple wood and brick, I pulled my phone from my pocket and read the 'No Service' indicator at the top corner. There was no God. Not here anyway.

"No cell service. No wifi," Henry confirmed. "You get used to it."

"I'm in Hell," I cried.

Henry laughed and hastily tried to cover it with a cough.

"I'm glad you find this entertaining," I muttered to him.

"Not at all," he said confidently and flashed a million-dollar-smile. He tilted his head and added, "Just try not to be like him," he said.

With a tilt of his head, Henry indicated another young man who stood out by the edge of the lake twirling a sword in practiced and refined movements. Like poetry. The blade flashed in the sunlight as if he wielded a star and not a sword. Or was *he* the source of the light?

Sunlight. It dawned on me again as I looked around. It was indeed daytime. Hadn't I left evening at my mother's?

Henry must have caught me staring at the sky or else he was reading my mind. "Don't try to make sense of the days here. I tried once, thinking it was similar to the time in Wales and that… was not the case."

"Whales…?" I asked. "Like… Killer whales?"

He stared at me. "Wales. Like… Are you messing with me? Like you did with Merlin?" Henry shook his head and raised his hands again as if to wave away the moment. "…You know what? Nevermind. We'll leave that for later," he said and shook his head. He had given up on me like the American education system had.

"So what was his deal?" I asked as we continued on toward the village. My hands were stuffed in my sweater pockets and I fiddled with my phone, rolling it over and over with my fingertips. I kept my gaze lowered. Henry knew the way, I only had to keep him in view. Or at least his feet.

"Oh," Henry said and I watched him try and retake his train of thought. "Gawain—"

"Gawain?" I snorted. "What kind of name is that?"

"His," Henry said seriously. "Gawain is the heir of, well, Gawain. He's Black Irish."

I glanced back at the one with the sword and returned my attention to where I walked. Henry had slowed down to my pace. I couldn't follow him anymore and I had to push my hood back to see him in my peripheral. "No…" I said. "I'm fairly certain that is by no means a black man. You're black. He's kinda whitish."

Henry laughed and it was a big laugh, straight from his soul. "No," he chuckled when he finally came down. "His ancestors left Ireland during the potato famine and immigrated to the United States. They were insulted by being called Black Irish since they were pretty mixed after a few generations. He wears it like a badge of pride."

"That potato famine thing was real?" I asked. I had always thought it was made up. I didn't understand how so many people died over rotten potatoes.

"Very real," Henry said, not questioning my terrible education. "Try not to bring it up, he gets weird about some things so I'm warning you now. He's a bit odd."

"I think you're all a bit odd," I muttered.

"You'll see." He didn't disagree.

We continued on down toward the little village and the banging ring of metal on metal assaulted my ears. The first building on the outskirts was the blacksmith, set away from others because the heat of the forge was unbearable even as we passed by. The man before the flames cracked hammer to metal and I winced every time that sharp *ting* hit my ears. He was a big man with big arms and a thick neck, a very frightening figure. And he waved to Henry like so many others with that same happy smile. Henry was obviously very well liked.

"So what is all this *heir* stuff everyone keeps talking about?" I asked as we passed and the sound grew softer in the distance.

Henry sighed. "That is something your parents should have told you about a long time ago."

"Imagine for a moment that they're pretty terrible parents and give me the quick version," I said.

"There... really isn't a quick version?" Henry said with uncertainty. "From your response to Merlin, you don't seem to have much background to base anything on."

"Humor me, Henry," I said flatly.

Henry stopped where he was. This was apparently too big for him to walk and think about at the same time. He crossed his arms and tapped his chin. He was broad chested and this didn't make him look any smaller. If he wasn't much older than me, why was he so broad? He looked like a muscled actor that was cast as a high school football player.

"So out in the world you came from, there's a myth," he began, "About a king that would rise again when the world needed him most."

"Zombie Airbender King," I commented. "Okay."

Henry winced. "It's... easier if you keep comments til the end?" he suggested.

I shrugged and let him continue.

"His name was King Arthur, and when he lived, he had a group of knights under his command, the Knights of the

30

Round Table. They sat as equals with the king and were considered the best in all the realms. In the simplest terms: we, the heirs, are the direct descendants of those knights." Henry finally looked at me.

"So it's not a myth?" I asked.

"Not for us," he told me.

I looked him over and said, "Heir of King Arthur, huh? Does that make you a prince or something?"

"Not to my knowledge," Henry shrugged. And resignedly he added, "Doesn't stop some people from treating me that way."

"And Gawain is the heir of Gawain," I said glancing back to the dark haired young man that seemed so focused on the sword in his hands that nothing and no one else existed. "And me?" I asked.

"Specifically, the heir of Galahad," he told me. "In more simple terms? One of the three heirs of Lancelot du Lac."

"Lance... a *lot*," I muttered. That was certainly a name.

"Lancelot had three children. One with Elaine of Corbenic, which resulted in the birth of Galahad. One with Queen Guinevere. And one with his wife, a Scottish princess named Iona," he told me.

"Damn..." I muttered. "Couldn't keep it in his pants, or what?"

"It's... much more complicated than that," Henry told me, and there was something in his voice, some kind of sadness as if these events were not some long ago story, but something deep in his heart that affected him every day. He spoke of these people as family, a family that made some terrible mistakes, or had some terrible situations befall them.

I pushed it to the back of my mind. It wasn't *my* family.

"There's been discussions as to whether we're the

descendants of these great men," Henry said, "or their reincarnations. Merlin says we are descendants. Though on occasion, we've all had dreams that aren't ours, seem to know things we shouldn't know. It's troublesome but—"

"I'll get used to it?" I finished for him.

"No," he shook his head. "But you'll learn to use it. I see it as a gift."

Henry was too optimistic. I couldn't hate him for it though.

We continued on and passed people milling about. No one appeared to be very busy.

"Does anyone do anything here?" I asked. The only person that had appeared to be working was the blacksmith.

"Today was supposed to be a day of celebration, for your arrival," he replied. "You put an end to that pretty quickly, so they're just taking the day as it is."

"Glad to be of service," I grumbled. I was glad they weren't swarming me at least.

He walked me through the village with fewer words. I didn't feel like speaking. Every time I opened my mouth people only gave me more nonsense to sift through. If I hadn't passed through the portal myself, I would have thought this was some strange and elaborate prank. Perhaps, it was a dream. I had been falling asleep in class lately.

I pinched myself. "Ow..." I muttered.

"I did that too," Henry said. "I think everyone does."

That was not very comforting considering the fact that it seemed as if he had been raised knowing he would end up in this place. Was it still all a dream to him? To everyone else as well?

At the other side of the village stood a small ring of houses. They were much closer together than the others and as we neared, I saw my father standing outside one of them. "What took so long, Henry?" he asked.

"Admiring the view," Henry lied. "The way the lake caught the sun was most idyllic. I imagine Nancy will have a painting of it by supper."

Henry hadn't been completely informal with me, but the prim and proper tone he used with my father made me skeptical, as did the fact that he did not hesitate to lie straight to his face. And for what purpose? I didn't pay too much attention to Henry's words, but at the mention of the name Nancy, my father's lightheartedness at our late arrival turned sour. He grimaced at the name. I had to meet this Nancy and be friends with her if this was how she affected my father. Yes. I made an oath to myself in that moment to be best friends with this Nancy.

"Thank you Henry, that will be all," my father seemed to growl his dismissal and he walked through the open wooden door and into the house.

When he was out of sight, Henry said to me, "I'll see you around." He bowed at the waist and part of me wanted to feel flattered. Overall, I was baffled and a little embarrassed.

Henry walked away then and the last thing I wanted to do was step inside that building. I stood at the threshold for a moment, staring at the rough wood flooring. My home with my mother was not grand, but it didn't look drafty. Taking a deep breath, I looked around for a place to run. I looked for any way to escape. Would the mere thought of fleeing be stopped by Merlin? My heartbeat was rising and my palms felt sweaty. I took a step back, my desperation for an escape forcing me to turn and twist, wildly searching about.

And then my eye caught it. Atop a hill was a crumbled pile of bright white stone and it basked in the sunlight streaming down from above. Feet moving without me, I was two steps away from the front door when I blinked. It lasted a lifetime. Laughter echoed around me, children, families. I heard the neigh of horses and the clash of sword on shield. When I opened my eyes, the rubble was no longer there. A grand castle stood upon the height. My heart sang at the sight of it, at the way the red banners danced in the wind.

The bag dropped once more from my shoulder and I ran towards the castle that beckoned me from above. If I did not reach those stone steps, did not stand beneath the light that poured through the windows of the citadel, I knew my heart would crumble to ash. I needed to see them. I needed to know my king was safe, that my brothers-in-arms were there waiting for me. I had to know that Camelot survived, that I had not fought for nothing. That I had not forsaken them...

Someone grabbed me. I blinked. Tears streamed down my cheeks and I fell back to the ground swinging. At first I fought because I needed to get to the top of that hill. I needed to know the fate of those I loved. And slowly, with a gentle breeze brushing across my skin, it all fell away. The fog in my brain lifted and I was swinging because someone had a hold on me.

"Stop. Stop! For chrissake! Stop!" she shouted.

I paused, frozen with my arms out wide like a toddler struggling to get away with two fistfuls of cookies and she finally let me go.

Bounding up to my feet, I stared down at her. She was taller than me, all legs. She was as tall as Henry, or taller, and her skin was darker than his, too. Her hair poofed atop her head in two puffs of tiny curly ringlets.

She stared up at me with brown eyes and said, "People don't usually start running for Camelot their first day."

"Camelot..." I muttered and looked to the ruins. They were

nothing but crumbled stone once again.

"Someone should keep an eye on you. You're an odd one," she said and rose to her feet, dusting off her tan trousers. She did not dress as casually as the others. She looked like she stepped out of the same place as Merlin with her outdated clothes and a faded blue tunic that would have been shapeless if she hadn't been wearing a worn leather belt at her waist. "I'm Eddel," she said and offered her hand.

"Socorro," I said and did not shake her hand.

She held it out a moment longer and then let it drop to her side. "I'm the heir of Perceval."

"Galahad," I muttered.

She smiled and it was beyond charming. "I know," she said. Her gaze left me and drifted out to the ruins on the hill. "I was the first heir to arrive. I've never seen anyone do that before."

I stared defiantly back at her.

"It's a lot to take in," she said, "and it's not easy."

"What isn't?"

"Living in their shadow."

We were descendants of knights. There was more expected of us, those who had been born as the heirs. My stomach roiled and my heart pounded in my chest. Anxiety flooded my mind. This was too much. Who was I now? Had I ever only been me? Or was I always destined to be the heir of Sir Galahad?

CHAPTER THREE

Tradition

The house wasn't so terrible. It kept out the cold even though it didn't look like it would. The rooms were smaller than I thought they'd be, mostly a single communal room without a dining table and two smaller rooms for sleeping. There wasn't even a shower, a toilet yes, but no shower. And even that toilet was more like a terrifying hole in the ground with a wooden seat over it. I would be crapping into the abyss.

The walls were mostly bare, with the exception of some old swords and shields. I preferred the house my mother decorated, with its vibrant colors and the salt and pepper shakers shaped like chickens.

This certainly looked like my father decorated it. It lacked soul, and so did he.

I dropped my bag into my room and found the bed left much to be desired. It looked old, like someone stuffed a burlap sack with grass and said good enough. And yet, when I sat on it, it felt softer than the bed I had at home. I wasn't sure I liked soft. At least it didn't feel like a grass sack.

My father hadn't wanted to talk to me. He didn't seem to want much to do with me at any other time of my life and that hadn't changed since my arrival. All he said to me was some grumbled directions and a few unspecific points of his hands. He was vague and irritating. I passed the quiet time in my room, staring up at the ceiling and trying to digest all that Henry and Eddel had said to me.

Eddel had walked me back to my house. "To ensure you don't get lost," she said with that charming smile.

She was delightful, the way she spoke was calming. She didn't expect any answers from me as she told me that I have free reign to walk around the village unattended. "Though it might be best to take someone with you for a few weeks. It is easy to get lost. All of the buildings look the same. If you do go out alone, as long as you can find someone, they will point you in the correct direction. They're all very nice."

That was something at least. Though, I didn't expect I would be leaving my room much out of personal preference. Avoidance was my key to happiness.

The sun began to set and I watched the sky outside my bedroom window begin to gray into dusk. The door to my room swung open and my father told me, "Dinner is ready, let's go."

There would be no privacy here. I imagined that if I closed that door too hard or tried to lock it, I'd lose the privilege of a door altogether.

Twilight had settled gray and solemn, and as I followed my father from the house I watched the world around us come to light with paper lanterns in the trees. They were stretched across wooden poles to illuminate the main paths through the village. Reds, purples, blues... More colored and patterned lanterns hung from the overhang of the roofs. Metal lanterns hung at the doors like porch lights.

"They're celebrating you being here and you've been

entirely ungrateful," my father grumbled as we walked.

The wonderment in my eyes darkened. I didn't want to take in the beauty of the lanterns anymore. I wanted to go back to my room and sleep until all of this fell away as one bad dream. I didn't want to celebrate. I didn't even want to be here!

Reaching up, I flipped the hood of my sweater over my head. The blinders were back and once more it pushed away everything and let me focus on the path directly ahead of my feet. My father completely disappeared in my eyes. If nothing else, that was a small victory.

The pavilion came into view, a grand open-air structure with old fashioned stoves and fire grills. People sat on numerous benches at tables that stretched out in four straight lines. There was little room to cut between the aisles and I dreaded the eventual walk between them. They were already filled with people. I didn't want to sit with anyone and mingle.

"Welcome Socorro," said the woman that served me a full plate. "We're glad you made it."

A wide silver cuff bracelet danced on her wrist. It was too big for her and when it settled it dangled precariously as if it would slide right off.

She was pretty, dark hair and olive-skinned with the lightest brown eyes. Even in the twilight hours, her eyes seemed to glow like light through a glass of whiskey.

I caught myself staring and managed a stuttered, "T-Thanks."

She gave me the kindest smile in return.

With plenty on my plate, I made a mad dash for freedom. Though it was less of a dash and more of an awkward, power walk from the front line to the end of the rows of tables where fewer people sat. I found a spot all my own with no one around me and took a breath as I sank onto the bench.

Grilled vegetables, potatoes, and a chunk of meat. I hadn't grabbed utensils, I was too busy trying to make an escape.

"Here," I heard and looked up to see Eddel. She held out a knife and fork and a shaker of salt. "Gawain's mother is a terrific cook, but she's always a bit underwhelming with seasonings."

"White people," I muttered as I took what she offered.

Eddel stood very still. In fact, she stood so still for so long that I looked back up at her to see if she was even still there. She bit her bottom lip as she watched me with withheld humor. Then she dropped down to sit across from me. "I'm going to sit with you," she told me.

"Why?" I asked as I began to eat.

"Because you're very funny, and very crude," she said. "And you won't draw so much attention to yourself if I sit with you."

Spoon of potatoes in my mouth, I turned it and let it hang between my lips for a moment. I slid the spoon from my mouth and asked, "What do you mean?"

"Everyone's dying to get to know you," she said. "You wouldn't want complete strangers flocking to your table while you're trying to eat, would you?"

"And you are…?"

"Not a *complete* stranger," Eddel said simply as she ate.

She had a point. That was something I certainly did not want. I would have preferred to be alone, but if I had to stomach the presence of one other person that seemed relatively decent then that was what I would have to do.

Eddel was interesting. I had to admit that much. She had a

39

more refined way of speaking. And though I couldn't exactly pick up an accent, there was something there, something that reminded me of the way Merlin spoke. It wasn't British English, and it wasn't American English, but it was pleasant nonetheless.

Unfortunately, Eddel didn't keep everyone away. She kept the more adult looking individuals away, the parents and the guardians of the heirs. She didn't keep away the heirs.

The bench beneath me shifted as another body sat down beside me. I couldn't see them with the hood of my sweatshirt still up and I looked to Eddel in time to see her sigh heavily.

"Quinn. Socorro," she said and gestured from the person to me. I didn't bother looking. "Socorro. Quinn, Heir of Bedivere."

"Which means nothing to you, right?" Quinn said. Another accent. It was familiar, flowing with rolling r's.

"Nothing at all," I said.

"Bedivere was—" Quinn began.

Spain Spanish? "Puss in Boots," I interrupted. Silence.

Eddel shook. She covered her mouth with her hand and her shoulder's only shook harder until she squeaked and then she threw her head back and laughed. Startled, I looked around. Everyone was staring.

I slapped the table in her direction and hissed, "Eddel!"

The bench beside me shifted and I glanced over to watch Quinn walk away, his red-brown jacket sitting close around his torso. Paired with his dark pants, I was reminded of something else that I couldn't put my finger on.

"You're terrible," Eddel chuckled.

"What?" I balked. "I was trying to—" My face felt hot and I sank down deeper in my seat. Pushing away my plate, I set my face on the table in its place and that only set Eddel off laughing again.

"Come now," Eddel whispered and I felt my plate tap the top of my head. "You have to eat something so we can sneak around tonight."

"What?" I muttered into the table. This was my first day and she was already talking about sneaking around? "Where?"

"Ah, that caught your interest," Eddel said as she leaned in. The table creaked. "It's tradition," she said. "Any time we have a newcomer, we always go out to the lake at midnight when everyone else is asleep. Are you coming?"

All of my skepticism must have shown on my face.

"You're not interested?" she said, her brows knitting close. She was saddened by the mere possibility of my refusal.

Did I want to meet everyone? No. Did I want to be in the house with my father? No. Did I want to show up at the lake and take the risk that there wouldn't be a single person there and I'd get laughed at for it? Definitely not.

"Not at all," I replied.

"Oh..." Eddel said softly. I couldn't help but feel as if I had truly upset her. "It's just... usually..." She shook her head and smiled. "Nevermind."

The smile ate at me. I ventured, "I'd hate to show up and no one be there."

Eddel looked at me surprised. Something like that had never happened to me before, but it was always a worry. So often people had told me one thing and never followed through. There was no reason for me to believe her when she said it wasn't the case. She was a stranger. I knew nothing about her.

"Then..." she began slowly. "What if I came to get you?

And I walked with you. If no one else shows up, I'll still be there for you to ignore."

Eddel got me. In that moment, I felt like she actually understood me. There was no pressure, just a suggestion. She wasn't saying she would hold my hand. She was saying she wouldn't let me face uncertainty alone.

"Alright..." I muttered and sat up a little straighter. "Fine. I'll go then."

"Great!" Eddel said excitedly.

I sank a little lower in my seat at the attention her happiness brought.

I was surprised when I looked at my phone that night, the screen showing 00:00. Midnight. Briefly, I wondered if that was the actual time, and if it was, what signal was my phone picking information from to accurately tell me it was time to go? Was there a magical satellite over the valley that said, "Yes, you can know time as it applies to you, but good luck communicating with the outside world?"

I stepped outside anyway with the hood of my sweater pulled over my head and heard a soft, "Psst!"

Eddel was there. She'd been waiting for me by the front door.

"Am I late?" I asked.

"No, right on time, why?" she asked.

"The time on my phone is right then," I muttered.

"That seems to be the case," she said. The magical valley satellite was working.

I walked with her into the village again. It was dark but the lanterns still hung, dancing back and forth in the gentle wind that kicked up and knocked back my hood. There was no reason to block everything out when I could hardly see anything at all. The night was thick all around us and if it weren't for something shining far ahead, I wouldn't have seen much of Eddel at all. Luckily, I was able to follow her silhouette. From behind she looked like the shadow of a very tall and fit Mickey Mouse with her two hair poofs.

There was no moon out. The sky above the trees was full of stars and none of them were constellations that I recognized. I had never seen stars so bright.

The short walk down to the lake had distracted me with sights and smells: the cool thick earth, the sweetness of the trees. I heard fluttering of far off insects. A perfect night for fireflies. Unfortunately, I hadn't seen fireflies in several years. Part of me blamed kids who put them in jars when I was younger. Bastards.

Soft blue light grew brighter and brighter beyond the trees until we stepped through the line of massive wooden trunks that protected the village from the lake. The water was placid, the only movement stirred by the gentle wind. A rolling slope led down to the waterside, but I stayed where I was, staring at the peaceful lake as I let the light wash over me. My heart felt full and once again I felt grounded. Blood pumped steadily through my veins. Air flowed in and out of my lungs. The world eased me, steady and sure in a way I had never felt before.

"Ready?" Eddel asked.

"For what?"

"To jump in," she said.

I laughed. "I don't think so. And don't tell me it's tradition."

"The Lady of the Lake tells us all something when we arrive," she said with a whimsical tone and a flourish of her hands. "Or, that's what we like to hope. No one's ever heard anything from the Lady of the Lake."

"With my luck, I put my foot in that water, the Lady of the Lake is gonna wake up and drag my ass to Hell," I said.

Eddel was grinning again, the light from the water illuminating her teeth. "You are a breath of fresh air," she said.

I felt my cheeks redden. People actually said things like this? It was embarrassing.

"Where's everyone else?" I asked.

"On the other side of the trees, right over there," she said and began to descend to the lake shore. Her shoes crunched through dirt and rock and then finally I heard the soft steps on a finer sand.

Hesitant to follow her, I wondered why I didn't hear any people. They were utterly silent if they were actually there. I didn't believe her, but I wanted to.

Against my better judgment, I followed Eddel down the slope. I kept my eyes on the branches that shrouded my view of the rest of the lake shore in leaves. My heart pounded in my chest. It was deafening. If she had lied to me, I didn't know what I would do. I paused briefly in step and wondered in that short moment if I should turn around and go back to my father's house.

And then... there they were. When I came into view and they saw me, many of them waved. There were so many of them, these heirs to the Knights of the Round Table. They too were dressed in sweaters, jackets, and jeans, protecting against the chill crisp air of the night and that errant wind that swept past without warning.

They were sitting, standing, a few quietly whispering to one another, but no one really talking. I didn't understand how so many people could be in one area simply waiting. It creeped me out. Though many of them had waved, none jumped to their feet. No one rushed at me and demanded information. There was no pressure to join them.

Just past them was a dock that looked fairly new, the planks straight and strong. I wondered if the building of this dock had angered this Lady of the Lake and that's why she refused to speak to any of them. The thought that she was petty made me smile.

Twice Eddel hadn't lied to me. It wasn't enough to entirely win my trust but it made me ask a question, "So you just... go in the water?"

"We all do," Eddel told me. "The newest person first, and then the rest of us follow."

"You realize this sounds like some weird cult baptism, right?" I asked her.

Eddel crossed her arms and stared out at the glowing lake. For a moment I thought I had offended her again. Her face was screwed and she seemed to be thinking. Then she nodded and said, "You know, we're all raised knowing about all of this, so we don't give it a second thought. But you do make a good point."

I stuffed my hands in my pockets and muttered, "You don't have to keep humoring me by pretending to be on my side."

I couldn't leave it alone, constantly throwing rocks at their ideology, doubting every person even when we seemed to be aimlessly meandering on the same side. In that instant, I couldn't stand myself. Standing on that silty shoreline, I stepped on the back of my shoes and slipped out of them. I peeled my socks off and stuffed them in my shoes with my phone for safe keeping.

To escape the awkward situation I had put myself in, I decided to march into the lake. Perhaps the Lady of the Lake would drown me and I wouldn't have to actually think before I spoke. Eddel was patient with me, but patience was never infinite.

Standing at the edge of the water, I looked down at the gentle ripple of waves as it lapped up toward my toes. This was dumb, but matter how I felt I had already decided to do it. I dug my hairy toes into the sand and as I took that first step, I wondered if the weight of my wet jeans and hoodie would actually drown me once I got too deep. I would be safer if I didn't go too far.

The water was warm and I gasped as my foot plunked into it. One foot on land, one foot in water and something churned within me. I longed for the ruins on the hill. My heart cried out for the stain-glass citadel and the light on the red banners that rippled in the wind upon the hill.

I left land against my better judgment. I slogged forward until the water sank through my clothes up to my hips. I kept my hands up, gliding along the surface as glittering droplets of water fell from my palms whenever the gentle roll of water left my touch. Shimmering ripples widened from beneath my hands, radiating from them, radiating from my body.

Knights of Camelot, I thought. I didn't know what that meant.

The stars overhead captured my attention again, so far and still so bright that I felt it wasn't a lake I swam in, but the universe itself. The lake was its own shimmering galaxy that reflected the purples, greens, and blues of the endless heavens above. If I drifted through space, then what was this world that I stood on? What was this strange place where time was different and so very much the same, where I could swim among stars. Was it magic? Had I decided to give in and truly believe… in magic?

I took a deep breath and dove beneath the surface. I wanted to know what trick this was, what kind of hoax awaited me.

Beneath the water, the glow was overpowering. I could see nothing. The endless light consumed me and I broke the barrier of air and water with a gasp as if the dive had stolen every bit of my breath. I should have felt… panicked. The warmth of the water called to me. Serenity flowed through me and I let myself float, my eyes on the starry sky once more.

There was no Lady of the Lake. If there was, she chose to speak to me the same way she had the others: not at all. Even without her though, I found satisfaction within her waters. I didn't feel alone. For once in my life I felt like I was exactly where I belonged, not under someone's foot, not being ignored on the sidelines. I wasn't a window to look through. I didn't feel small as I drifted through the universe.

Splashing and laughter brought me back to the present. I lowered my body into the water and looked back at the shore. I had drifted far from them, that once quiet crowd that had waited for me. A smile crossed my face. I knew them. Even if I didn't know their names. I knew them from another time, another place.

One arm in front of the other, I swam back. I tread water when I saw Eddel with a group of the others. Dread filled me for how inconsiderate I had been. When she saw me, that small cluster fell silent. They all bobbed in the water like me, except Eddel. She was the only one that was tall enough to touch the bottom so far from the shore.

An eternity seemed to pass until Eddel finally offered me her hand. I took it. I didn't think twice. The water around us came to life with that white glow I had seen beneath the surface. Gasps filled the air. We looked at each other and one of the boys beside her took her hand. The glow spread to him. One by one we linked hands and arms until every person was touching. The luminescence spread away from us as if we were an oil spill on the ocean and it grew until it encompassed the entire lake as far as I could see.

In the distance, mist seemed to recoil at our penetrating light. It rolled back at the base of an island. There were trees. I could smell sweet apples. The island was coming to us, revealing itself to us.

Someone yelped and all at once the lake went dark and the island vanished in the night.

"Nancy!" a chorus of shouts went up.

"I'm sorry!" came the distressed reply.

My cheeks hurt. I was smiling so hard. Before I knew I was doing it, I was laughing. I was laughing in a way I wasn't sure I had ever laughed before, the way Eddel did it. The way Henry did it. With every part of my soul. My laughter was filled with humor, surprise, excitement. I was excited about something! This was magic. This place, these people, everything around me held magic and the world vibrated with it. I could feel it!

Laughter sprang up around me, either laughing at Nancy, or the fact that the lake had shown us all something together that none of us had seen before.

"Alright!" someone cheered. "Knights of Camelot, class of 2018!"

I only laughed harder. It felt like a graduation, like I had passed some kind of test only meant for me. I felt validated that my existence meant something. I imagined… we all felt that.

The lake felt surreal. I didn't stay in the water for very long after the island vanished back to wherever it had come from. Gathering my things, I took a seat on the shore. They were all so easy with one another. Everyone was in the water and I wondered how they could stand to be so close to one another, how they could handle the noise.

The longer I watched, the more I realized it wasn't as utopian as I first thought. There were groups that ignored one another, some played a little rougher than others. Some of those shouts were in anger. And there were two young women further away from everyone else, quiet and content with only one another's company.

Dripping water and footsteps in the silty shore caught my attention. At the edge of the lake, a young man stepped out in shorts and a gray shirt that clung to him like a second skin. He was leaner than Henry, but he had the same strong musculature and I wondered if there was a mandatory gym class that they all attended.

He shook himself like a dog and his wet mop of hair flung water in every direction. I lifted my hand to block my face.

"'Ey!" I complained.

"Oh," he saw me and gave me a grin. Half of his face was in shadow, the other half illuminated by the lake. "Sorry Il— Socorro." He had stopped himself from calling me Ilar and pointed to me with both hands. His fingers bounced up and down as he lifted his head and seemed to be repeating my name. I could see his lips moving but he said nothing aloud.

Rolling my eyes, I looked away and that was when he came and sat beside me. He drew up his knees and leaned forward, crossing his arms upon them. "Gawain," he said and offered me his hand.

I shook it limply. In Texas, that was a hanging offense. He

merely took it as it was intended: uninspired.

He sat quietly for some time and then asked, "If you could choose one song to describe yourself, what would it be?"

Slowly I turned my head and looked at him incredulously. "What?"

"Any song," he said. I hadn't misheard him.

"I don't know." Why would I know? People didn't have theme songs like movies. "Do you have one?" I shot back at him.

"I might," he said, "I'll tell you when you tell me yours."

"Not interested." I shook my head and turned my attention back out to the lake.

A little quieter, he said, "I've got one for all of us."

My eyes widened at the whispery sound of his voice and I glanced back at him. This kid was weird and he was leaning in toward me with eyes full of excitement and mischief.

"Something Wild. Lindsey Stirling featuring Andrew McMahon," he told me. He must have thought I was giving him attention. I wasn't.

Abruptly, I snapped, "Never heard of it."

He made a small, "Hmm…" of amusement and was quiet again.

I tried to think of every song I knew. Which one was me? But just like when someone asked me my favorite book, or food, or movie, it all ceased to exist.

"I Hate Everyone, Get Set Go," I said. That had been the last song I had listened to that morning before school. That morning? Technically this was a new day but it still felt like a short lifetime ago. At least a few weeks.

Gawain slowly turned his head to look at me, but the movement had been stiff and mechanical. It was off-putting. Even more so because the shift put his face in full shadow.

He could see my face in the blue light of the lake and I couldn't see his. "Nah," he said and shook his head. He leaned back on his elbows and continued, "Nah, I don't think so."

"It's my song," I huffed, "You can't tell me what my song is."

"Alright, alright," he gave in easily. "Maybe it'll change."

"Maybe not." I was sticking to it even more since he didn't like it.

"This place changes people. Mostly for the better."

"Did it change you?" I asked.

"Still working on that."

Despite myself, I was curious about this odd duck. "Your song?" I finally asked.

He didn't hesitate. "Hate Me. Blue October," he said.

"Rock on, emo kid," I nodded. I knew that song. I knew that song very well. Music was an interesting thing. We were complete strangers and we still knew how that song *felt*.

He chuckled, "Yeah."

Sometimes people listen to a song for the lyrics. Sometimes just for the sound. I always thought that people who listened to lyrics were a little more advanced than those that didn't. Don't get me wrong, meaning can still be derived from absolute gibberish. (What does be-bop-a-lula even mean?) But I always imagined that when someone told me to listen to a song they loved, a song that reminded them of another person, a place, or an event, that it was a gateway to a piece of their soul.

"Everyone have a song?" I asked.

"Some of them have told me," he shrugged, "Most ignore the question. I think of songs for them anyway. Everyone has one."

"Everyone?" I asked a little slower. Gawain nodded. I tilted my head as I considered his confirmation. "So is the song describing them, or how you feel about them? And is it the lyrics or just the title? Because you could say Hard out Here by Lily Allen is Merlin, but Champagne for My Real Friends, Real Pain for my Sham Friends by Fall Out Boy is how you feel about him."

"Wait..." he muttered, his brows knit and his lips parted. "Are you going by the titles or the lyrics...?"

"See how that can be a problem?"

A beat of silence passed between us as he stared frozen at the lake, one brow raised and an expression settling on his face as if his universe no longer made sense.

He snorted.

Gawain laughed. He dropped flat on his back and covered his eyes with his hands as he kicked his feet in a fit of giggles. I grinned. It wasn't that funny, but I was mentally patting myself on the back for a job well done.

Those nearest to us in the water began to stare.

"Nothing to see here! Carry on!" I called out and waved my hand at them.

They shared glances amongst themselves and were slow to move their attention away from us. Henry had said that Gawain was odd. I realized that I had joined the club. That was okay. It seemed... fun. I hoped that meant people left me alone. Gawain seemed to get his uninterrupted moments to swing around a sword in the sunlight. If only I could be so lucky.

Humor finally dying down, he tucked his arms beneath his head like a pillow and told me with a smile that I could hear in his voice, "The ones I pick for others are how I think they are. The lyrics."

I drew up my knees and hugged them close to me as that chilled errant wind blew over. My clothes were still wet and I shivered.

"Cold?" he asked.

"Nah," I lied.

Laying flat, he brought his legs up and flung himself to his feet. I stared. I didn't think people could actually do that outside of a movie. "Well I'm cold," he said, "so I'm going back in. See ya later, Sox."

"*Sox?*" I balked. "Fuck you *Guh*-waine!"

"Ha!" he laughed over his shoulder as he walked away from me, "Like I haven't gotten that one before!" He sprinted the rest of the distance between me and the lake and flung himself into the water with reckless abandon. Those nearest to him complained and they started splashing one another when he surfaced.

Once again this was something that I couldn't quite bring myself to attend. I had made an appearance for this so-called tradition, and that was enough. I was glad I had managed to avoid the welcome celebration. These strangers were overwhelming. An entire village of them would have been too much.

My excitement over what we had seen at the lake took much less time to pass than I thought it would. Seeing something so fantastical, I should have wanted to understand it more, to know what that island in the lake was. I didn't thin much about it at all after getting out of the water. My curiosity was hand been spent on Gawain and I was feeling much too cold to sit and ponder any longer.

I took to my feet with my socks in my hand as I slipped on my shoes. Wet shoes were bad. Wet socks were a hell known by all, but walking in wet jeans would be upsetting *and* chaffing.

I didn't know if I could find my back to my father's house in the dark. I was pleasantly surprised to find that the path came to me as if I had always known it and any other trail in this quiet, hidden place. When I walked through the front door, I closed it softly behind me and turned around to the sound of a struck match. Light erupted to life and the orange glow of a candle illuminated my father's stern face. He sat in the main room, his feet propped on whatever our equivalent of a coffee table was.

"Did you have fun?" he asked. That was a loaded question. I didn't trust the growling tone in his voice. It scared my heart still in my chest.

"These motherfuckers don't even have electricity?" I tried to deflect the question. Though, my statement was true enough I hadn't noticed before when the sun was up. No wifi, no fans, no air conditioning, no modern conveniences of any kind. I was in a renaissance faire at the mercy of a deranged wizard.

"Watch your mouth," he snapped.

My heart leapt into my throat. I stood as still as I could possibly stand. I wanted to disappear, to be a window. I needed him to look through me and not at me.

I swallowed and my throat hurt to do it.

"Your outburst at dinner was disgraceful," he said with a cold, distant tone. I would have preferred the growling, biting words that meant I still had a chance to escape. He was putting distance between us, dissociating from the fact that I was even his child.

My brows raised in curiosity. He could have barged in my room at any time after dinner to yell at me, yet he waited for me to come through the door in the middle of the night. Had he come home at all after dinner? I was beginning to think he hadn't. I knew where I had been. Where had he?

"And sneaking out." He rose from his seat.

"It's tradition," I said evenly as I fought the urge to step back. Don't move. Don't draw attention. Be a window.

"There is no such tradition." His words were punctuated with steel.

My feet moved, I flinched. I wanted to reprimand myself for showing weakness, for not grounding myself and being brave and standing my ground but I couldn't do it. Not when he looked at me the way he did, not when my knees knocked together and my body trembled. For all of my bravado, I was nothing against him. "The lake!" I cried out. "The lake, we went to the lake!"

He took a step and I froze. If I moved, he would come after me. If I moved, it would warrant discipline.

"You went to the lake?"

"Y-Yes…" I stuttered.

Tears stung at my eyes. If he saw them fall, he would only be more enraged. He would say this was no reason to cry and if I needed a reason to then he would give me one. I couldn't cry. I couldn't run. If I ran and he caught me, there would only be hell to pay. I had only ever run from him once in my life and that… that was a grave mistake.

He strode toward me. "You waste of—" He reached for me. *Run.*

That word echoed through my soul and I didn't argue. I hit the door before I flung it open and I fled into the nearly pitch black night. Tearing past the trees, my clothes rubbed my thighs raw, my feet slipped inside my shoes. My socks were long gone. I was going home, my real home. My mother couldn't save me, but I would feel safer hiding in my room, even if I knew I couldn't hide forever. He would get me eventually… but I could get away for just a moment. I could save myself for a few minutes. Maybe I could last a whole day.

I reached the stone steps that led up to the circle of white arches and I launched myself up them. Merlin had shown me how to use the portal when I arrived and I was going to use it again. Staying in this place with my father as my guardian was impossible. I couldn't live with him. I wouldn't. I would never be truly safe. This rich and wonderful, magical world could all go to hell if it soothed my anxious heart. This place was too good to be true and I didn't deserve it anyway. I wasn't what they thought I was. I wasn't an heir to anything.

Running into encircling arches, struck my hands on the nearest stone. Nothing happened. I slapped it again and closed my eyes. *Home.*

Nothing. Maybe that wasn't the right one? Did it have to be a specific archway? I searched desperately trying to remember which one I had come through from my mother's house.

"Home…" I muttered as I slapped my hands on the next archway. "Home. Take me home!" I shouted as I struck another. The white stone scraped at my palms and as I begged the next column to send me back to my mother, I left streaks of red as an offering.

The ugly tile flooring. The old couch. The orange light in the kitchen. Try as I might, home would not form in my mind. I had spent my entire life there thinking about how ugly it all was and when I needed it most all of my imagination had abandoned me.

"Ilar!"

His voice echoed and I fled to the furthest arch, desperate

for one last chance. I clung to the pillar, banging at it with my open hands, pleading until I heard his boots clip sharply on the flagstone floor. Time was up. Chills ran up my spine. Every hair on my body stood on end. My mouth was dry and I didn't want to look. I didn't want to see it coming.

Each step he took was louder, drowning out the sound of my heart as terrible silence filled my body. His movement was deafening, echoing. I couldn't breathe.

"That's far enough Erik." English. Male. I knew that voice.

"Henry," I exhaled. My legs felt weak. I glanced over my shoulder, but as I tried to turn around my knees buckled beneath me and I sank to the floor.

Henry was there, and so was Eddel. Henry's voice had brought my father to an absolute halt and the only sound of movement was their bare feet across the stone. They dripped water with each step they took to cut off my view of my father. They cut off his path to me.

"This has nothing to do with you, Henry," my father said. He stood tall, squaring his shoulders. I was his problem to fix. Not theirs.

Eddel responded first. "Socorro is a Grail Knight, Erik."

The kind, amused voice she gave to me was gone. She was serious, commanding. She and Henry were noble and held themselves as if they were royalty. She *was* taller than Henry.

"Regardless if she is a Grail Knight," Henry said, "she is the heir of Galahad, a knight of Camelot, and above all else, one of mine. It is obvious that you cannot control your temper."

"Henry—" my father tried to speak. He was immediately interrupted.

"There is blood on the stone that condemns you," Henry raised his voice. He wasn't quite shouting but the authority he held made my father flinch. The heir of Arthur had power, real prince or not.

Eddel said, "As of tonight, you have lost your ward. You are unfit to be a guardian."

"You can't—" he balked.

"We can," Henry said evenly. "We are." Not a threat. A promise. Whatever the hierarchy was, my father was not at the top of the ladder. Not this time.

"As you are one of knight's blood," Eddel continued, "we cannot strip you of your home. So Socorro will stay with me."

"You are dismissed," Henry declared.

I caught a glimpse of my father between the two of them. His face was bright red with anger. I doubted he appreciated the reprimand from children, especially two black children.

Stiffly, he gave a short bow of his head and departed.

Together, Eddel and Henry turned to me. They did it the same way, their heads bowed, their gazes dragging across the floor before raising up to land on me as I sat bleeding and crumpled upon my miserable self. Nonthreatening. They knew how to communicate with their entire bodies, not just their words. It was strange. It made me feel like I was some kind of animal that they didn't want to frighten. In a way, I was.

"When you're ready," Eddel said softly, "the three of us will get your things and I'll take you to my home."

CHAPTER FOUR
The Code

I don't remember grabbing my things. I don't remember the short trek to Eddel's house. I don't remember anything other than stripping off my wet clothes and throwing them somewhere around the room right before I collapsed on the bed. I vaguely remember Eddel tucking me in, but whether or not that was all a part of my overactive imagination, I don't know. Either way, I tiredly pulled the blanket over my head and pretended I no longer existed.

The lake was a beautiful place that was forever ingrained in my memory, but when I finally awoke the next day I smelled like grimy, disgusting, sludge-eating, bottom-dwelling fish. The Lady of the Lake needed a housekeeper.

Draping the scratchy wool blanket over my shoulders and pulling it tightly around my grungy body, I shuffled out of my room. Only when I stood in the open doorway, bleary eyed and half asleep, did I immediately recall that this was not my mother's house.

"Good morning!" Eddel called out and then amended, "Actually, it's almost noon now. But that's okay, you had a rough night."

Eddel was a mom friend. I had never had a mom friend

before. Just a mom.

"Gawain came by," she said. "Brought your wayward socks and a note. Don't worry, I didn't read it. Not that I understand half of what he says anyway." She pointed to a dining table in the middle of the room where my rolled up socks and a folded piece of yellowed parchment lay. She had an actual table, unlike my father.

Eddel had more than a table. She had art. Her home looked like a museum. There were old shields and swords, but there were banners and tapestries, too. Numerous heraldries were fixed to the ceiling at the top and bottom hems like an old historic quilt. She had paintings and sculptures. Eddel's home was beautiful.

"I brought breakfast," she said. "It's a little cold, but if—"

I cut her off.

"Shower," I croaked, my throat ached with the morning. No... not the morning. I had been screaming. My mind flashed back to beating my hands on the stone arches. I clutched my blanket and hissed at the aching pain that radiated up my arms. I focused on that for a moment and let it ground me in the present. I used it to pull me away from my own mind before I spiraled. Over the course of my eighteen years of life I had taught myself how to forget what had happened; how to push it away and bury it, laugh at it and keep going.

I ran my fingers of my right hand over the palm of my left and felt gauzy cloth wrapped around it. Someone had bandaged me up. Both hands had been cared for. They were the cleanest part of my body and I didn't remember it happening at all.

"Oh," Eddel said slowly, dragging it out a moment as she considered my singular word of interruption. This was not the Eddel my father had met last night. She was bright-eyed and bushy-tailed, as my aunt on my mother's side used to say. Her two-poof hair had been transformed into multiple tight poofs all over her head. She was cute in her belted shirt and over-worn trousers. Same kind of clothes, different colors. I wondered briefly why she didn't dress like everyone else.

"Well," she said, "you can go dressed in your blanket but it might be a bit scandalous."

"Scandalous?" I grumbled.

"Community bath," she informed me.

It was my turn to say, "Oh... Right." I had wondered where the showers were.

"Get dressed and I can walk you there, be sure to take a change of clothes with you."

I didn't argue. I really wanted a bath and there was nothing in this place that was going to stop me. I returned to my room and dressed in my damp clothes from the night before. They were cold. They were disgusting. I wondered how terrible my hair looked.

As we walked, dirtied blanket in my arms—since she said we might as well take it for cleaning—and my clean clothes in hers, Eddel told me about the baths. They were Roman-style baths. That would have sounded really nice... if I hadn't studied history. Though she assured me that since many of the heirs weren't used to the lack of privacy and the oddness of oils and moving between pools, there was another option and that was an actual tub, but I would have to haul the hot water myself. She said, "Most have gotten used to the different pools by now. Even the knight's blood are lazy."

She took me to a private bathing room, showed me where

to take the bucket to fill it with hot water, set my clean clothes on a shelf and told me, "Set your soiled ones outside and I'll see to it that they get laundered."

Laundered… It sounded like a strange word.

I nodded and went to it.

I didn't have the arm strength to lug around buckets of water. I did say I was a skinny, knobby-kneed individual, didn't I? My arms were toothpicks and I carried the bucket high in front of me, my elbows out sharp to either side as I did a strange paddle-foot shuffle back to my bathroom in an attempt to not spill the water. It didn't help that my hands ached with the slightest pressure against my palms and the rope handle bit into the scrapes and bruises.

When the bath was halfway full, I got one last bucket and set it beside the tub. This was good enough. I didn't have the strength to lug a single extra water droplet. After a short few seconds to regain my strength, I stripped down and dropped my clothes outside like Eddel had told me to.

I was glad to see that there was modern soap. Sure they could make soap, but one or two of the heirs had apparently protested that they were expected to change too much too soon. Merlin allowed them to bring a few toiletries. Merlin had not given them toilets. Merlin was not well liked for that. I preferred the way Eddel told that story. It was funnier. I still hated Merlin for giving us abyss holes in the ground to crap in.

Clean rags to bathe with were a godsend, but instead of throwing myself into the hot water, I used the bucket I had left at the side of the tub to wet myself down and scrub at my skin. I wet my hair and used a bottle of shampoo that Eddel had given me, rinsed, and then conditioned. When I ran out of water to rinse with, I dipped the bucket back into the tub.

Only when I was clean and free of soap did I slip into the tub and take a good soak. This was what I wanted. Hot water on my legs, on my lower back, soaking into the scrapes on my hands. The water didn't come up very far, barely over my thighs, but I bent my legs and slid my back down into the bottom of the tub. This was not a comfortable tub for bathing.

While I sat there, I began to wonder... Did the water from the Roman baths come from the lake? Or another source? Were people soaking and swimming in lake water? My face scrunched in disgust at the thought.

It didn't take me long to start to feel a chill and I pulled the little plug at the bottom of the tub. I got out to the sound of the water rushing into a drain in the floor and I chuckled at the thought that it might flow down into the lake. Eat my bath water, Lady of the Lake.

I draped my towel over my head and took a deep breath. Reaching for my clean clothes, I paused. I had completely forgotten to pack razors in my bag when I left home. I groaned, though I was glad I hadn't brought shorts to change into today. I had packed shorts for this excursion of an unknown duration. I would get to them eventually. I just hoped I had a chance to be presentable when I did.

Dressed in a blue shirt and jeans, I slipped on my warm dry socks and my luckily-not-still-wet shoes and gathered the toiletries I had brought. When I stepped out, Eddel was waiting for me. She held a new blanket in her arms.

"Sorry that took so long," I apologized.

"Oh you're fine," she shook her head. "I was talking with Henry anyway."

"Are... you and Henry... you know..." Why had I even begun that sentence? Curiosity? They were close, but so were most of the heirs.

Eddel looked at me and her brows raised. "Not at all," she assured me with a very straight face. "No one here is… romantically involved in anyway with one another. Merlin forbids it."

"Forbids it?" I asked as we began our descent back to her home. I wondered how well a bunch of young adults were adhering to that rule.

"Oh yes. To keep the number of heirs the same. We've lost many over the years. Down to seventy five descendants of knight's blood now," she said."

"How does that work exactly?" I asked. "Don't people usually have multiple children? If my dad had two kids, wouldn't we both be the heirs of Galahad."

Eddel shook her head. "Nope. One ancestor, one descendant. Those are the rules."

"What about Lancelot?"

"That was the start of a lineage, before Arthur's death. Merlin created this place after Arthur's body was sent to Avalon and every descendant that lived came here when they came of age," she said. This was their fact. They could not mix bloodlines so they grew up in the outside world, learned to understand it, and when it came time to have children of their own, they ventured out again.

"So everyone before us are the heirs of somebody?" I asked.

"Nope," she said, "Just us. The… What did Gawain call it last night? The Knights of Camelot, class of 2018? Those of us born at two-fifteen in the afternoon."

"Why two-fifteen?"

"The time that Arthur died at Camlann," she said matter-of-factly.

There was too much information here to take in, an entire life that I didn't know I was supposed to have. "I guess I should pick up a book or something and read about this stuff," I sighed.

"I... don't recommend that," Eddel replied and shook her head.

"What? Why not?"

"Merlin frowns on it—" I cut her off with a loud sigh. Merlin again with his rules. "Let me finish," she said.

I took a deep breath and stuffed the blanket under an arm so I could put my hands in my pockets.

"Our parents tell us the stories of King Arthur and the knights of Camelot. We're raised on them, on the knight's Code of Chivalry, on everything we're expected to be. That being said, Arthurian legend is a subject that the outside world knows about as well. Scholars over the ages have written of it. It has passed through so many hands, through so many ideas that the stories have become skewed. The French hated the British and Galahad rose in importance. The British hated the French and wrote that the fall of Camelot came from Lancelot's adulterous relationship with Queen Guinevere. It's a mess."

That made sense. The story here was different than the ones outside.

Eddel continued, "We are kept far away from these stories. Our parents are supposed to guide us to our truth." And abruptly she said, "And that is why Gawain is strange."

"Excuse me?" I came to an abrupt halt and stared at her with furrowed brows.

"Gawain slipped away from the teachings," Eddel said as she turned to me. "He became enthralled with the tales from the outside libraries, the adventures of his namesake. There are things said in these other accounts that convey a... different Sir Gawain than we know. It tore our Gawain apart to learn these things. It still tears at him but he's gotten better over the years. He came to this sanctuary earlier in life than the others and time here has helped tremendously."

I stared at her. What had he read? How could reading a book mess someone up? ...Aside from the 1999 masterpiece The Mummy.

I shook my head. I didn't really want to know. If it had made him the oddball that everyone else saw then I didn't want to share the same fate even though I was already joining him on the 'weird kid bridge' where we talked about sad emo kid music things together.

"Music is his coping mechanism," I muttered.

"It's his safe place, and his way of acting out," Eddel said. "No one here knows music and lyrics the way that he does. At least, no one that wants to admit to it."

I understood that. Something had happened to Gawain and music helped him deal with it. Then, he leaned into it a little too hard to feel... in control of something. That was his thing that made him feel like an individual, it made him *Gawain*.

I did things like that too. I think everyone does.

One thing I thought I had escaped by coming to this magical place was school work. I was considerably further behind than my peers when it came to understanding who, what, and why we were whatever we were. Little did I know those lessons would take form with Merlin as my instructor. As Eddel led me through the village after breakfast, I was looking forward to sitting in a class with other heirs. I could get to know them a little better. I could hide in the back of the class and avoid getting called on altogether.

"Everyone else has lessons of their own," Eddel said and my hope was crushed.

Merlin was going to be my own private tutor and I would be the center of attention. Terrific.

We passed a large group of our fellow descendants of knight's blood and I watched them in their staggered, spread out rows as they drilled through sword techniques with none other than my father at the head of the class. If I was going to ever catch up to them, I would have to deal with him and sharp weapons eventually. I didn't like the idea of either of those things at all.

The other heirs... they were so focused, their movements sharp, their attention forward. I had never seen such intensity. As I passed by with Eddel, Gawain's gaze shifted to me and he gave a smile and a short wave with is free hand. I saw my father approach him. Gawain didn't notice he was there and a short *whack* on the back of the shoulder with the flat of a short sword made Gawain jump back into place. The glare I received from my father made me hide behind Eddel.

"I wouldn't worry about him," Eddel told me. "While he is the most experienced swordsman we have in the sanctuary, you will be training with Quinn's mother to hone your swordwork."

That was a blessing. The last thing I wanted was to be on the receiving end of anything else my father had to teach.

"But first, someone has to get you caught up on The Knight's Code and a little history," she said.

"Can I please just not today?" I heaved a sigh. "I've had enough new trauma to last a lifetime. Can I go back to bed?"

"You'll get into a routine soon enough," she assured me. She wasn't giving in at all. And since she was stuck with me as an unexpected roommate, I went along with what she wanted me to do. What was my other option? She'd saved me from my father, given me a place to sleep, made sure I had food. She included me in all the other reindeer games when I was the weird little red-nosed freak in Santa's pasture.

I groaned. "What if I don't want to get into their routine?" Because I didn't. Not even a little bit. Not at all.

"You'll at least find a routine of your own."

Somehow, I wasn't too sure about that. I didn't do well in school in the outside world, how was I going to do any better here?

Eddel led me up to a building about the size of her house—my house—and knocked on the closed door. There was nothing special about the place. The outside was as brick and thatch just like every other building, with larger stones closer to the foundation.

Merlin answered the door and held it open for me. The moment I stepped across the threshold, Eddel said, "I'll see you later then."

"Wait, what?" I balked.

"I have lessons of my own," she said. A polite, charming smile graced her lips "You'll be fine. We all know you can hold your own against Merlin."

She was teasing me... How rude.

The old sorcerer grumbled, "Don't give her any ideas Eddel."

"I wouldn't dare," she replied to him and I thought I saw a quirk at the corner of her lips, a hint of mischief that hadn't sounded in her voice. There was more to her than I originally assumed. Why wouldn't there be?

I couldn't pinpoint it, but I was correct in my previous

thought that there was something similar about the way they spoke. A particular flow of their words, a cadence in the way they thought. It was almost musical, and mildly unsettling. I wanted to know why, but I wasn't about to ask outright. Not there and then.

"Alright you," Merlin said a little more forcefully and closed the door.

Eddel's departing figure disappeared from sight and a lump of uncertainty formed like a knot in my stomach, rising up into my throat with bile. I tried to calm myself. My safety net was leaving me and she wasn't coming back. I was alone.

I took a deep breath and tried to count backward from ten. None of my anxious thoughts were true. Merlin was not the enemy. Eddel was not my only acquaintance and she wasn't abandoning me there forever. I was scared and had allowed myself to lean on the idea that I could cling to her for support and that she was always going to be there. From one crutch to the next, finding ways to hide and people to lean on... I couldn't do that. I had to stop doing that. None of them were going to save me every time I was in trouble. Last night had to be some kind of fluke. There was no such thing as a hero, and Eddel and Henry weren't mine.

Turning to face the room, I found the far wall covered in old time-stained maps. Curious, I ventured closer. The yellowed parchment showed me the world as I knew it, but some things were slightly different. Names of places had changed. There were markers on cities I knew of that held notes of things I had never heard of before.

"United Albion," Merlin said and I swept my attention back to him. "United under Arthur Pendragon, King of Camelot. The once and future king."

I opened my mouth to speak and he raised a hand to

silence me. Half a day here and he was starting to catch on to my quirks and habits. I didn't know whether to be impressed that someone was paying attention, or terrified.

"I know," he said softly. "This means nothing to you." His eyes glistened and I retreated a step closer to the map wall. My knowing nothing saddened him. When he looked at me, he saw his world fading away. His friends were vanishing before his eyes. Everything he clung to had begun to dissolve and I was proof that no one outside this village cared.

"Eddel said you had lessons for me?" I said and crossed my arms.

"No need to posture here, Socorro," he told me. "No one is here to fight you."

I didn't think I was posturing. In hindsight, I was. Crossing my arms made a boundary between the two of us and I needed armor to protect myself when I didn't know how else to.

Once again, I opened my mouth—this time to protest—and he held his hand up to silence me. I dropped my arms in a huff and shoved my hands deep into my pockets. Of course they were women's jeans, so my hands folded into fists and were still barely covered by the absurdity of women's fashion.

"Arthur's Albion is a thing of the past," he admitted. "But Arthur is not. And we are not. Galahad's blood runs through you. You are an heir. These two things are not up for debate. This is your truth for better or worse."

His words should have put me on edge. They didn't. I knew what he said was true, just as I knew that I didn't have a choice in this matter. I was the heir of Galahad. I carried his legacy and this was something only I could deal with, as my blood was not the same as the other heirs.

Henry had mentioned having dreams that weren't his own, but I had had a vision. The glittering castle on the hill didn't exist, neither did the clash of steel and the laughter of people that had rang through my ears. What I experienced was my own to deal with, just like Henry's dreams were his own problem. I didn't know how to handle this and I guessed none of he other heirs knew either, but I hoped that this time spent with Merlin helped me understand. Something had to make sense.

Quiet, Merlin watched me. I wasn't running away this time and that saddened expression that had found a home on his face had slowly begun to uplift. "We will start first with the Knight's Code of Chivalry," he said and gestured to two seats in the middle of the room. Those two chairs had not been there when I had first entered the room and aside from them and the maps on the wall, there was nothing else. This was the oddest classroom I had ever been in.

"Code of Chivalry?" I asked. "If a weird guy with a fedora and a neck beard pops out and calls me *mi'lady*, I'm going home to my mom."

Merlin's bushy white brows raised in curiosity and he slowly replied, "No…"

That was another small blessing at least.

"There are seven rules in the Code of Chivalry. You will be expected to live by them," Merlin told me, "In the same way that the other heirs will."

Will, he said. Did they not live by them now?

I couldn't promise him anything, not without knowing what it was he asked for. I also wouldn't promise such a thing regardless. Old rules rarely applied to the current world. The Bible was a perfect example of that. My mother liked to read the Bible, and she often went to church. My father claimed to follow it. That was bullshit.

"The first," Merlin began and gestured to the seat and I took it quickly, more than eager to get this over with.

"Never do outrage nor murder," Merlin said.

That was easy enough. I didn't fight people and I certainly wasn't large enough with my scrawny chicken-leg arms to do any kind of murdering. I knew what I wasn't capable of. In short, that was everything. Fighting and murder, however, was probably at the top of the list. Pretty sure I was incapable of learning a second language and ice-skating, too but physical altercations and being a cause of death ranked significantly higher.

"Second," Merlin said, "Always flee treason."

I opened my mouth to ask a question and he spoke before I had the chance.

"The wording of this seems lost on your generation," he told me. "It does not mean commit treason and flee from it, as Quinn and Gawain were so adamantly convinced." He huffed. "It means to flee the belief of it. Never to commit treason against king or country. And before you try to interrupt me again. Yes, you do have a king."

I sat quietly with my hands in my lap and he stared long and hard at me, as if daring me to open my mouth. I gave him a short gesture of my hand to continue. I could keep my mouth shut a little longer, though that didn't mean my thoughts were silent. Inside, I was laughing at Gawain and Quinn's mutual assumption. As far as having a king, however, I wasn't sold on the idea. I didn't vote for him.

"You are never to be cruel," he said. "But you must give mercy unto one whom asks for mercy."

Had my father taken this oath? Had he sat through this class with Merlin and ignored his every word? I let the thought pass. This wasn't the time and this rule was straightforward enough. Simply put, don't be 100% a dick.

"Always do ladies, gentlewomen, and widows succor," Merlin said. He made a face and then added, "It has come to my attention that this is very sexist in your age and that you should give succor to all in need."

"You're going to need to define that word," I said as I slowly shook my head, "because that's not a very flattering word."

"Help," he clarified. "The word means help, aid, assistance, and it is what you are expected to give to all who require it."

"Especially damsels in distress," I smirked. Unless my damsel was in distress in another castle... then she was on her own.

"I find it interesting that this is what you snort at considering succor is the word from which your name derives, Socorro."

That little smile that had been growing on my face slid completely away. I let Merlin continue uninterrupted. He had won this round.

"Fifth," he continued. "Never force ladies—Anyone. Never force another." He had corrected himself this time and it earned him a raised brow of curiosity.

Never force. Everything must come willingly here and that was something that made me grimace. Was I not being forced to be here? Or was it again that these rules did not apply to anyone but the heirs, and if so that was entirely unfair. Why were we held to standards higher than any other; standards that those that guarded and guided us, that raised us, did not seem to be bound by.

My jaw tightened at my realization.

"Do not take up battles in wrongful quarrels for love or

worldly goods," Merlin told me. "The only fight worth fighting is for king, country, or God. Do not fight otherwise."

Regardless of what he said, I did not see Arthur as my king. Camelot was not my country. And as for God. What had he ever done for me? I wasn't sure I believed in him—or her—but I was sure that if I voiced that to Merlin, his head might explode. There was only so much I imagined the old man could actually take. Seventy-some odd heirs of Camelot might be pushing his hold on sanity.

"And lastly," Merlin sighed, "you must fear God, and maintain his church."

I stared at him. He stared blandly back at me.

The old man blinked slowly. Once. Twice.

"Excuse me?" I snorted and covered my nose as I laughed. "You want me to do what?"

"Yes, yes... all of you are a bunch of heathens. Why have most of you laughed at that?" His face reddened.

"We just..." I shrugged. "Religion isn't a huge thing to me?"

Merlin stared at me as if I had slapped him across the face and then danced away. Part of me assumed he already knew my stance on the Christian God, and religion in general. I didn't know who would have told him. The only person whom might have known was my father and him knowing anything about me at all was not a bet I would take.

"But... you are the heir of a grail knight," he said softly, carefully. He sounded so... lost. "God means nothing to you?"

I shrugged, holding my shoulders by my ears for a moment. "Firstly, I don't know what that means. The grail knight thingie. And secondly... I mean. I just don't see how or why I'm supposed to show allegiance to some omnipotent being that has pretty much screwed me. I didn't want to be born, I didn't ask for it. And as I recall, you didn't even approve of my parents making me so what the fuck does it even matter?"

My voice... it sounded cold and distant to my own ears. I was bitter, and strangely enough, I was on my feet. I didn't remember standing during my speech. I hadn't necessarily been heated in my response, I should have been able to moderate what I said and how I said it. It was as if my brain had momentarily switched off when the words came tumbling out.

Merlin silently watched me. His hands were clasped before him and he stood so still that I thought he might have become a statue. I was sure it was in his power to do so... The way he stared at me with a soft gaze, I had his complete attention. He hadn't responded to my outburst and while the look in his pale blue eyes was not aggressive, it still made my stomach lurch. The impulse to run rose within me. My heart leapt into my throat and I risked a glance at the door. The last time I had taken my eyes off of someone in a stand off, I ended up running for my life.

"If you are scared of me," he said, the words rolling past his lips. He spoke softly and I held my breath to even hear him at all. "You may leave."

The air in my lungs exhaled in a rush. The door was right there. I could escape if I needed to.

"I-!" I bit back the word. It had come out too loud, too fast. I wanted to say I wasn't scared. I wanted to scream it. "I am scared," I finally whispered. "But I... I shouldn't keep running. Right?"

"Correct." He nodded and held his head bowed for just a moment.

I wasn't his Galahad. I wasn't someone he knew and I wasn't raised in the security of knowing this place waited for me one day. He seemed to finally be understanding that I was different, even though I hadn't wanted to be. I was broken. I was made... wrong.

We stood in silence for a short moment. I felt like this was a pivotal shift in our relationship, actually taking a moment to be in one another's presence without demands and without fear. Merlin did feel safe. He didn't make my skin crawl and he didn't make me feel like I was a burden. At least not yet.

"You have time to settle into these rules before I ask you to be bound by them," Merlin finally said, "Even Eddel has not taken the oath."

That was a relief. This made it feel more like a trial run, applying the oath and adapting to it. Though, some of those rules were going straight into the trash can. There were some things I was fairly sure that I was incapable of.

"Merlin...?" I asked softly. I was having trouble finding the words. "The... last night? When we... when the heirs went down to the lake? Is... that actually tradition?"

"It is *your* tradition," he said. "Eddel wanted to start something to bring together the heirs. When a new one arrives, everyone goes down to the lake in the middle of the night. She said all of you needed something that was just your own. Something rebellious. Something fun. That all of you were children, after all and that it was nice to feel like one, especially when no one was watching."

"So that's why my dad knew nothing about it..."

"It is not his world to know," Merlin said. "Your father is... a proud man. He has always been the strongest, the fastest, and the bravest, but that was never enough and he never seemed to understand why."

I stood a little straighter. I hadn't realized I had been slouching, my shoulders rolled forward as if I were ready to creep out of the room but Merlin's words were a comfort. This world was not my father's, it was mine. I was an heir. He wasn't. I had power here. He did not. I was ruining the thing he wanted most in his life and I never wanted it in the first place. He was angry with me because of this. He was angry because I was not better, because he was not better, and nothing he could attain would ever be enough for him. I would never be enough for him.

"Merlin?" I said softly.

Merlin blinked and his expression was kind as he tilted his head. He was listening. It felt strange to not be on guard in his presence.

"What's going to happen to my mother?"

"She is well," he reassured me and I believed him. "The other parents left outside the sanctuary take care of one another the way that we do in here. They may not be allowed here but they are not forgotten. The heirs do return to their previous homes from time to time."

My father was garbage that often lied to me. Why would Merlin think that trust was easy for me?

The old sorcerer smiled broadly and reached out to pat my shoulder. "Socorro," he said softly. "You are safe here. You are the children's children of my oldest friends. There is nothing I would not do to keep you safe."

I thought I was tough. I could block out anything, push past it, run from it. I could ignore everything and anything...

Merlin broke me.

I cried again. Not the way I had when fleeing my father. Not the way I had when I said goodbye to my mother. I didn't understand where it came from, the relief I felt, the wholehearted trust that I had in Merlin to protect me. Everything would be okay. The old man embraced me and I cried into his robe, crushing the fabric between my fingers as I gripped it tight against my face.

"If you blow your nose on my robe, I will make you fart toads for a week."

I laughed. I buried my face further against him and laughed until it hurt, until I cried again and then gave myself hiccups. The sorcerer patted my back. For the first time in my life, I felt like I could exist without being told that I was doing it incorrectly. I wasn't weak. I was just a kid.

This was a place of healing. I had only been here for a day, but—like Gawain—I was on the path to feeling better. Maybe one day this place might become some kind of home for me, even though I was still appropriately skeptical as to what living here required of me. I wanted to be hopeful.

CHAPTER FIVE
Sense of Self

Merlin called our first lesson quits after my little breakdown. When I stepped out into the light of the afternoon, my chest felt tight. I wanted to know more about these people, their stories, and if they felt as conflicted as I did being the heir of some long gone knight who might still have some influence on our lives.

Metal clanged in the distance, a quick strike and ring and the rows of students in my father's sword class abruptly halted where they were and seemed to flee in the same direction. They had been called to lunch like a bunch of cowboys on a cattle drive. I had seen a few western movies like that.

"You coming?" I heard and glanced over to see Gawain standing a few yards away.

"To what?"

"Lunch."

So I was right.

I shoved my hands into my pockets and drew up my shoulders as I joined him on the walk toward the pavilion. He broke the easy silence when he asked, "Sooo... How're you feeling?"

"Keep It 100. 3For3," I muttered after a short moment of contemplation.

Gawain walked a little straighter. He stared out ahead of him and I watched the wheels turn in his head. He squinted, and I didn't think it was from the light. Gawain blinked slowly, licked his lips, and said, "I don't know that one. We should trade music."

Reaching into his back pocket, he pulled out a small dark green MP3 player with matching green earbuds and held it out to me.

"All I have is my phone," I replied. And I had left that in my room.

"It's fine," he shrugged.

In the normal world, I wouldn't have taken it. I would have stayed in my bubble and ignored the offer, especially since I didn't really know him or when I would be able to get it back to him. This time, I took the MP3 player and put it in my pocket.

"Keep it safe," he said with a smirk, "it's all I've got."

"I'll guard it with my life," I said monotonously and gave him a little thumbs up.

Gawain smiled. He then stretched his arms high in the air before he locked his fingers behind his head. "Alright, I don't know that song, but I feel like you're being sarcastic."

I chuckled, "Yeah a bit."

His smile broadened into a great big toothy grin.

"Keep it up, your face is going to get stuck that way," I snickered.

"That'd be nice for a change," he mused. He glanced down to me and I certainly had a curious look on my face. "No one's ever played."

I didn't understand what he was saying. I might have

missed a cue where he switched the subject. Smiling would be nice for a change, but when I spoke to him he was always smiling. The Gawain I met last night was a fun-loving guy. Eccentric with music, sure but not exactly what I would call weird or odd the way that Henry and Eddel did. I definitely knew stranger people in high school.

As we walked on in silence, his words kept running through my head. No one had ever played. Played what? His music game? Why not? How self-involved were people here that they couldn't be bothered to listen to a little music?

I went through the lunch line behind Gawain in silence. He didn't try to make me talk anymore. No one did. I went to sit in my spot at my table. I had only had one meal there but it was mine and no one else was there when I got to it. Gawain didn't come with me, he sat closer to the front with a bunch of other boys. I hadn't had a moment to myself since waking up and as I sat down, I grabbed the MP3 player out of my pocket. After a moment of being disgusted with the fact that I would be sharing earbuds with someone I didn't know—not that I would share them with someone I did know—I put them in my ears and set the first song to play as I started eating.

This was Gawain's personal playlist. This was the music he used in his everyday life and it almost felt… intimate in a way I never knew existed. Knowing someone's music is to know their soul, and as I sat there eating lunch, I realized behind that cheerful smile was someone who was entirely lost. It wasn't that there was neither rhyme nor reason to his music. My playlist was filled with very similar songs and a lot of the same artists. I knew why I listened to them, what I heard in their lyrics. And if Gawain heard the same things in his own music, he was as scared as I was.

This was Gawain's vulnerability. If I shared my music with him, would he see something similar in me? Had he chosen not to sit with me for fear of what my face would show? How would I have looked at him when the first piano note of The Black Parade hit my ears. Joy? Heartache? I had so many questions but what I needed to do was stop thinking and just listen.

This was Gawain: noble, self-sacrificing, humorous and afraid. If I could get over myself, I believed we might actually have a chance to be good friends.

I listened to his music throughout lunch, and even when I had finished eating, I let his songs guide me as I took my plate back to the line. Everyone around me strode to the lively tune of Misanthropic Drunken Loner by Days N Daze and I snorted back my laughter at the bridge in the song.

Gawain paused at the threshold of the pavilion and glanced back at me. He was leaving alone. The people he had sat down to eat with were all gone and he was by himself once again. He caught me with a dumb smirk on my face and he grinned and gently bowed his head. His long shaggy hair slid forward to cover his face and he rocked back on his heels and spun around with so little grace that I thought he would careen off balance. Instead he loped away to return to sword practice where my father awaited the heirs-in-training.

A tap on my shoulder made me jump. Beside me was a woman her dark brown hair in a braid over her shoulder. There were wrinkles at the corners of her eyes. She was old enough to be my mother, but she was built like she could take my father in an arm wrestling match without blinking. This woman brought the guns to the gun show. If ever there was a brick house...

I slowly pulled the buds from my ears and made sure to

turn it off before stuffing it in my pocket. The wires would probably tangle. That was a problem for future me.

"Hey Socorro," she said amicably. She had such a pleasant smile, and her words were as unaccented as mine even though she rolled the Rs in my name like a pro. "Valeria," she said and offered me her hand. "I'm Quinn's mother."

"Oh," I shook her hand. This was Puss in Boots's mom? I snickered at the thought that he picked up his accent from watching too many Antonio Banderas movies.

"He gets it from his father," she said with a shrug and I stared at her. She had read my thoughts, or at least my face. "I've had to explain it almost every time a new heir shows up." She gestured ahead of her.

I didn't take the lead. I had no idea where we were going. We walked side by side away from the pavilion and she told me, "I've lived here most of my life. After my mother died, my father brought me to the sanctuary. When I was old enough, I left and traveled the world. I met Quinn's father in Spain. He almost hit me with a scooter... Not entirely sure what I was thinking, but I ended up carrying his kid. And he surprised the hell out of me by telling me he wanted to be a part of our lives. He even tried to marry me. Can you believe that?"

I had not been expecting her to continue sharing her story. There wasn't a ring on her left hand. She didn't wear any jewelry at all. And by the way she spoke of 'Quinn's father', he was not her husband.

"I wasn't the type," she explained. "So I had Quinn in Spain, and was a terrible mother, bouncing back and forth in his life unexpectedly but usually only for holidays, until he was old enough to come here."

"Why are you telling me this?"

"You're an heir," she shrugged. "You should know about the people in your village. I'm not the best parent, but I'd like to hope I'm a half decent person."

I frowned. "Merlin approved the match," I said. "That's why you had Quinn."

She nodded shortly and didn't say a word.

"Does anyone here have any control over their lives?" I muttered.

She held up her hand and tapped her bare left ring finger with her thumb. "In small ways," she replied. "Things here are very conservative. Get married, have a kid, bring it here. Adhere to the Code. It's a very masculine society, and one thing you will learn quickly—if you haven't already—is that the female heirs are from unapproved parentage. Either love matches, or lust."

I was fairly sure knew which one my father's was.

"What I'm trying to say," Valeria continued, "is that you have an uphill battle ahead of you. They expect a lot from you, especially as a grail knight. Your father Erik became a different man the day he found out your mother was pregnant. He was one of our finest swordsmen. If any of us were ever destined to be in the place of you heirs, it was him."

"And now?"

She smirked. "And now, I'm here to train you. And I hope one day you're strong enough to knock him flat on his ass."

I wasn't sure I heard her correctly. If Valeria was saying my father deserved to have some one knock him upside his head and beat him at his own game then yes, absolutely I agreed with her. But if she was she training me to do that specifically? I didn't like it. The idea of being a pawn in someone else's game, even if I agreed with the outcome didn't sit well with me. If I was going to best him, it couldn't be in revenge. Wasn't it part of that Code?

Do not take up battles in wrongful quarrels.

The words came back to me like a song I had grown up with. I knew those words. To learn for revenge would stunt my growth. My pride would take a hit if I failed. My anger would flare; wrath would take hold like an infection. I could see that path as if someone had played it on a movie screen while I watched. If my father wanted to fight with me, that would be his pride on the line. Eventually, I would have to face him but it would be on my terms when I did.

I opened my mouth to ask a question: if this place spoke to everyone the way that I felt it was speaking to me, like a nagging in the back of my head. My aberrant memories were one thing but that wisp of words was like a guiding light, throwing relief and answers to me when I needed them most. I wanted to know what it was.

As I walked beside Valeria, I realized I didn't have a way to even describe it. This, like the memories and the lake tradition could have been something that only belonged to the heirs. Would she even know anything about it?

Closing my mouth, I took a deep breath and changed the subject. "So where are we going?"

Valeria led me away from the village where the buildings and trees fell away behind me and opened up to a great meadow. This was the place I had run to when I first arrived, where Eddel had pulled me away from my mad dash to the broken citadel. Tentatively, I risked a glance at the mound of white stones on the hill. This time it was nothing other than mossy rubble. There was no pull within me, no urge to run to it and I wondered for a moment if something was missing. Nothing felt wrong.

Maybe this was still head trauma from falling at school?

"Alright," she said abruptly and came to a stop where the grass seemed shorter. Not only was it shorter but it had been trodden into dirt with only a few sprigs shooting up here and there from lack of recent use.

I spun about one direction and then the other. This was a circle. The feeling I thought I was missing when I looked upon the ruins of Camelot crept up from deep within my stomach. My shoulders felt tight. My hands clenched and unclenched at my sides. This was a practice ring and even though I knew what we would be practicing, it didn't ease the unease that flooded my brain.

Valeria entered the ring and placed her hands on her hips.

Slowly, I drew a deep breath and stood straighter: shoulders back, chin up. Curiosity flashed over her face. Her eyes narrowed as she studied me.

"Well that's interesting," she said softly.

"What is?"

"You seem different. Just now, you had a look on your face like…" She shook her head.

"Like what?" I pushed.

"Quinn does the same thing on occasion. Like it's him, and not him. Like it's someone else," Valeria said.

"Someone else?"

"Your bearing," she answered. "Like it belongs to someone much older and far wiser."

Like a knight, I imagined she wanted to say, but also didn't want to completely freak me out. What did any of them really know about knights other than what had been passed down, and what Merlin told us. All it took was one person changing the narrative and then the entire story was corrupted.

Did I believe all I was being told was lies? No, and I wasn't going to trust blindly. I had never done that before. I wasn't going to start just because someone treated me well.

"Now..." Valeria caught my attention again. She smiled pleasantly and asked, "How's your focus?"

"Terrible," I replied. I had no reason to lie. I suppose my focus was a little better here since I had no phone reception. I would have so many unanswered text messages the next time I had signal. That was a lie. Maybe five, all from the same person. It wasn't that I lacked friends in the outside world. Sometimes we didn't talk, or didn't need to. Those were the best kinds of friends, the ones that could say everything to with a simple look. Nearly telepathic friends.

"Socorro?" she said my name and I snapped back to the present. "You weren't kidding..."

I smiled sheepishly and ducked my head. My shoulders rolled forward as I put my hands back in my pockets.

"Okay okay, no more of that. She snapped her fingers at me as she approached. "We need to work on your bearing and your posture. You slink around like a dog who's been hit with too many rolled up newspapers."

"I what?" I balked.

With a finger, she tapped up my chin and then crossed behind me. I tried to turn with her and she gently pushed my shoulder to keep me from following her. Behind me, she pulled back my shoulders, tapped my feet further apart, and poked my elbows until I let my hands hang at my sides.

Standing in front of me once again, Valeria crossed her arms and looked me over with consideration. "I mean... I guess it's a start."

"You have more faith in me than I have in me," I said and crossed my arms. She snapped her fingers and didn't have to say a single word when she pointed at me. I knew what she wanted, and with a rebellious sigh, I dropped my hands at my sides again.

"Do you dance?" she asked.

I laughed, an obnoxious little, "Ha!"

"A simple no would do," she muttered. After a moment, she finally began again. "Swordplay is a dance," she explained. "The best knights have always been masters of courtly behavior, game, and warfare. One thing your father never teaches is how integrated all of these things are. And who you are, your strengths and weaknesses, they will always show in them."

I frowned. Riddles, again.

She stepped forward and tapped my shoulders back again. "Stop slouching," she chastised.

I groaned. I didn't realize I had slumped at all. Maybe it was the mere mention of my father that took the wind out of my sails and made me want to be smaller.

Valeria smiled brightly. "Your insolence is refreshing," she chuckled. I started to protest and she cut in, "I'm not mocking you. You don't seem to really want to be here, and everyone else does. The other heirs are willing to step up and step forward and you... what is it you want?"

My mind flooded with answers. I wanted my father to have been around. I wanted my mother to not have to worry about work, about the house, about being deported because my father never married her. I wanted to know I wasn't crazy for feeling like I might want to be here. I wanted to know the truth, about everything: history, my history, their history. Why I was truly pulled to those ruins and why I was the last heir born. Why did the lake glow? What had we seen in the water and what did it mean? What was a grail knight and why did it have to be me?

Why does it have to be me? The words felt like they echoed in my head.

"I want—" I began sharply and the anger fell away. I didn't want to be angry. I wasn't upset at all. I wanted... "Peace," I said.

Valeria looked at me again that same way as when we arrived in this circle: perplexed and almost in awe. Did they not think that I was capable of complex thought, of introspection?

"I want you to do something for me," she said after a moment. "Walk around. Go about the village, go in the woods. Take a walk on your own. There is nothing here that can or would harm you. Merlin has seen to it. Find a quiet place to really take this all in. I don't think we've given you a chance to really get your bearings here. Tomorrow we'll start anew."

"Can I go up there?" I asked and pointed behind me to the ruins of the castle.

"It's best you don't," she said quickly, shaking her head. "No one has been there since King Arthur's time and Merlin wants to keep it that way."

"So... you want me to walk around and what... meditate with the trees?" I asked.

A broad smile crossed her lips. "Whatever you want."

I stared at her. This didn't feel like a trick.

"I'll see you tomorrow," she said and gave a quick bow at the waist before she turned and left me standing there.

I had the rest of the afternoon to myself. I wanted video games and pizza, not to hug trees and be one with nature.

CHAPTER SIX
Galahad

Quinn's mother, Valeria, left me standing out in the open. I shuffled my feet in the circle of dirt and tapped the toe of my shoe against a sprig of grass that tried to grow up into the practice ring that had been cleared by use. The afternoon was mine to do as I pleased and as much as I wanted to walk back into town and crawl into my bed in Eddel's house, I decided that maybe it was time to explore a little. Nothing could hurt me here, that was what Valeria had said. Merlin protected this place. They even called it the *sanctuary*. That meant safety. At least it did in the dictionary.

Reaching into my pockets, I went for the the headphones and paused. This wasn't the time to listen to music, I needed to listen to this world, his world. I was the descendant of this… Galahad person. This place was magic and I was supposed to be able to feel it. I needed to truly feel it. I needed to understand it.

Deep breath in. Deep breath out. I put one foot in front of the other and set off into the tall green grass of the meadow. I ran my hands along the tops of the thick blades of grass. They were soft as they tickled the tips of my fingers like down feathers. They slid over the clean, gauzy wrapping

Eddel had placed over my bruised and wounded hands after my bath.

Thick, musty dirt. Warm grass. The heat of the sun on the land around me. Sunlight had a smell here, the same way night had a smell. I remembered the way the starlight felt by the lake, the way the gentle breeze over flowers and cool earth quieted in the dark of night.

Each step felt like the earth was waking up beneath me. Not that I made the grass grow or the flowers bloom but life vibrated with energy. I felt this world and it felt me. My clumsy steps felt grounded. I strode with confidence. Heel, toe. Heel, toe. I knew these lands, the grass and the trees. I had walked this earth ages ago. I was merely coming home.

A forest rose around me. The grass vanished as the thick canopy above shuttered out the light. The gentle wind I had come know swept up the scent of the afternoon and I felt the light peek through the leaves and dot my skin. My gaze drew up those tall tree trunks and it was only then that I smelled that mustiness of moss along the bark, along the ground. I knelt, my knee touching the damp dirt and I pressed my fingers against soft green moss along the base of a tree. It felt like rain drops were falling under my skin, pattering against my bones.

Boots tread softly across the dirt. I looked up and saw a young man passing by. He couldn't be much physically older than me but his expression made him seem exhausted beyond his years. He wore armor. He was fair of skin but he had seen much of the sun. His soft brown hair caught the sun's light coming through the leaves the way mine had. Over his shoulders was his cloak, the bright red of Camelot pulled back from his left shoulder where the plates of his armor held the raised crest of a dragon.

He paid me no attention and as he continued to walk. I rose and fell in step behind him. That cloak billowed in front of me and I could feel the weight of it as if it were on my own shoulders dragging me down. I felt it shift behind me with each step that I took. I felt the armor, the heat and sweat between the padding and my skin. The plate metal on my shoulders was rigid along my back. It didn't fit well, but the chain links of the maille shirt was more than comfortable. This was a day trip, enough to be prepared, but not outfitted for serious combat.

A day trip... We were supposed to be on the lookout for him. For *them.*

My thoughts rattled around in my head. I felt disjointed and touched my gloved hand to my temple. Gloves...? Since when...?

I blinked and when I looked before me, the young man was gone and there were two others seated at a campfire. A pair of rabbits roasted over a spit and I could smell the charring meat and hear the sizzle of grease as it dripped into the fire.

The two men noticed me standing there. They glanced between one another and shared a look of concern. Their attention returned to me and one of them grinned so playfully that it seemed exaggerated and comical. He was a jester, not a real one. He was a soldier like me, seasoned beyond my years, but the mischief glinted in his brown eyes at the same time that a feeling of annoyance crept up my spine.

"Galahad," he said to me, drawing out my name. "Feeling well? Have you had any luck?"

Of course not. That was the reply. I didn't say it, but they continued on as if they had heard it. I wasn't feeling well. I had not had any luck at all in any of my endeavors. I was...

upset.

"Such terrible luck," sighed the other man as he stretched his legs out before him. Just looking at him where he sat I could tell he was tall. Much taller than me. Much taller than Galahad. He was a mountain of a man, though he wasn't at all intimidating with his pleasant blue eyes and his casual smile. I knew that smile.

These were my friends, my mentors. Why could I not recall their names?

"I wish we did not have to patrol," the first man dramatically lamented. He didn't want to be here at all. Neither did I, this was a farce to anyone with two brain cells moving fast enough to squeak together.

This is not a patrol.

It certainly didn't look like much of a patrol to me. They sat preparing to eat a late lunch while their horses grazed lazily nearby. Neither man nor beast wore a single mark of hard riding. All three of us were much too clean to have been out for very long.

"We *could* patrol," said the second man, "but to what end. We know they are far beyond our borders by now."

I do not like this. We should be closer to the queen at a time like this.

The first man shook his head. Dark tendrils of his hair— escaped from the tie at the nape of his neck—danced around his face. "Barely a man and already the most serious of our comrades."

Gawain. This was Sir Gawain. I knew it in my heart. I knew the mischief in his eyes and the reasons he drew upon humor at a time like this. He was so far from his home, from the other half of his soul.

"Do not be so hard on him," the other knight teased. "All of

Camelot is hunting his father."

This was Sir Perceval.

He is a fugitive.

The words were plain. I could not care any less for my father, for Sir Lancelot, and his dash for freedom with his beloved Princess Iona. I didn't know the man. He had not raised me and I had no sympathy for the bewitchment that had befallen him. I did, however, feel terribly for Queen Guinevere and the sorcery that had ensnared them together.

"I bet they are headed to the sanctuary of the Black Spire," Sir Perceval said with a nod of his head and then he glanced to Sir Gawain with a sly, suggestive smirk. Everything felt so dismal but we did our best to keep our hearts from sinking. Even if it meant poking at one another.

At the slightest mention of the broken tower to the east, Sir Gawain's face flushed bright red, and so did his ears and his neck. He cleared his throat and looked away from his fellows.

That humored voice in my head announced, *We could always go knock.*

"What?" Sir Gawain balked. "No. I... We can't do that."

I would like to know the story of the retaking of the Black Spire straight from the source.

We had switched subjects. I welcomed the levity that eased the uncertain pit in my stomach.

"I *am* a source!" Sir Gawain shot back. "And Perceval was there as well."

You should make an honest woman of her.

Sir Perceval bit his lips to keep a grin off of his face and he stared up into the trees as if they were the most interesting grouping of leaves he had ever seen in his life.

Sir Gawain wilted at his side. He looked absolutely

miserable.

What is wrong?

That was the question from a man that knew exactly what was wrong and had the intonation of a jerk.

Perceval bit his bottom lip. His innocent blue eye landed on his comrade and he asked, "She still will not have you?"

Gawain groaned and set his head in his hands.

"Will she not even entertain the thought?" Perceval blurted.

A pair of gossiping hens.

"Oh misery, Perceval," Gawain snorted. "I have not even asked her! She is content as she is. What use has she of me if she already has the world in her hands and those... tower dwellers at her beck and call? What am I?"

Expendable, it seems.

That was rude.

Sir Gawain groaned in agony and dramatically pitched himself onto his side. He lay upon his back and gazed up at the canopy high above as if entirely lost to his miserable fate. He set the crook of his plate-covered arm over his eyes. It didn't look comfortable and after a second, he dropped his arm back to his side with a huff.

He was a grown man, and still a boy.

"Oh get up," Perceval laughed, slapping his ankle. "You keep this up and she will demote you to the traveling Black Spire troupe."

"Oh shush!" Gawain waved his hand. "You had fun as well as I!"

That exciting?

"Galahad," Gawain grumbled, "You would not know the meaning of enjoyment if it bit you on the—"

"Gawain!" Perceval snapped and was immediately on his

feet. He truly was a mountain of a man and he looked past me, over where Galahad's shoulder would have been. He wasn't reprimanding the other knight, he was calling him to attention. That tone did not belong in the voice of such a kind man like Perceval and it put me on edge.

I turned. Neither Sir Gawain nor Sir Perceval had drawn their swords which made me feel that if I were careful, bloodshed could be avoided. I looked across my shoulder to where a man approached us. There was no reason for villains of this time to dress like one, but there was nothing else he could be. When I looked upon him, I knew his face and I saw nothing but a traitor. Distrust rose up within me like fire in my vein and my hand dropped to the hilt of my sword.

"Ease, my friends," he said, raising his empty hands to show that he was no threat.

I knew differently. Galahad knew differently. Sword or no sword. Weapon or no weapon. This man was dangerous.

How dare you show your face within the borders of Camelot. We search for Lancelot, but we should be hunting you.

"Galahad, we were friends," he pleaded as he approached me. "I only came to speak."

I drew my sword and held him at point. He stopped in his tracks with my blade mere inches from his throat. His deep blue eyes darted down the length of my sword and his brows drew together in sadness. When those dark eyes reached mine, they widened in surprise and a careful, hopeful smile surfaced on his lips.

Whatever this was, this… memory, this illusion, it played tricks on my brain. He didn't look like he was smiling at Galahad. This man did not seem like he was connecting to a lost age. He blinked slowly, curiously, and I swore that he was looking at me, at Socorro Apemlyn in the year 2018.

My throat felt dry but I somehow manage a partial, "Hi…"

An involuntary chuckle choked out of his throat as his bottom lashes brimmed with tears.

It was you.

Galahad found his voice again.

Your treacherous ties with sorcery bewitched Queen Guinevere and Lancelot.

The man swallowed hard. He breathed deep and lowered his hands at his sides. "That was human error," he said, returning to the moment with the knights before him. "You should know to err is human, Galahad. There are none close enough to God to escape error."

That was angry. Those words were bitter.

The slide of steel caught my ears behind me. "That is enough Mordred," Sir Gawain said. "Lancelot would never willingly leave Iona. That was his vow. It is the same as my vow to—"

"Merely words," Mordred snapped. "Actions speak much louder, do they not?"

Anger. I felt anger rise within me. I had trusted him! I had brought him to Camelot and he had betrayed me. He had betrayed all of us!

Mordred's eyes narrowed and I felt his gaze on me once more. "Why won't you *do* something?" he pleaded. Not to Galahad.

"*What*?" the word passed my own lips at the same time I heard Galahad speak it in my head.

The sun shone brightly and a gentle wind brushed back my hair. I took in the smell of the afternoon and tilted my head back to see the light spilling through the dancing leaves above. Everything washed away.

The knights were gone. Mordred was gone. There was no

more smell of cooked rabbits, nor horse sweat, nor leather. There was no sadness in Mordred's eyes, no pleading in his voice. No anger in my heart, no violence like a rancid pit in my stomach. There was nothing except the quiet of the forest.

The gentle rustling of the breeze through the meadow grass caught my ears and I wrenched myself from that moment. The first steps were fine, I felt nothing unusual other than my own uncertainty of what I experienced but with each following step, the sound grew louder and the pounding of my heart threatened to drown it out.

Before I could stop myself, before I even knew what I was doing, I was running.

The screaming sound escalated and transformed into the clash of blades, steel upon steel. I reached the open plain and there was silence again. The war in my head ended at the treeline. There was no battle when I spilled out into the grass, staggering with my hand clenching at my rocket-propelled heart. I had run toward nothing. Ahead of me on the hill were the ruins of Camelot: white stones glistening in the afternoon sun.

"Merlin said no," I shakily whispered to myself when I felt my body try to move again without me.

Merlin be damned.

Galahad. That voice. That voice that wasn't a voice but was a feeling coursing through my veins, that was Galahad. He resonated within me. How could that be Galahad if I was supposed to be his heir? Was I not? Was I something else?

"This is my body," I choked out. "I will not go and you cannot force me."

Silence.

He could not force me. This was part of the code that he

had sworn an oath to uphold.

"The hell is going on..." I exhaled. I felt tired, beyond exhausted. My legs didn't want to take another step and I dropped to my knees there in warm sun. I needed to rest. I needed to think. I needed to go back to bed like I should have done right after my bath that morning.

CHAPTER SEVEN

Growth

I had closed my eyes for what I thought was only a few seconds. The grass became softer. The dirt cooled beneath my legs. Even though I had fallen asleep, I hadn't dreamed. I hadn't been asleep long enough to dream anyway. At least, that's what I had thought.

I stirred, turning over and pulling my blanket up over my nose. Sunlight poured through my window and across my eyes. I groaned. I felt tired and sore and the sun was perfectly angled to annoy me.

"Hey... There you are," I heard in Henry's gentle voice.

My eyes flew open. My heart leapt into my throat and I shot upright in bed, or I tried to and collapsed back to my pillow. Every muscle felt weak.

"Henry...?" I squeaked.

He sat in a chair at my bedside between me an the window and he leaned forward, his hand lightly setting on the back of mine. "You're safe," he told me.

"What are you doing in my room?"

The sunlight behind him began to darken his features. I was quickly losing his expressions but I could still make out the careful dip in his brows and the tight smile on his lips.

He seemed worried. Why was he worried?

"It was my turn to watch you," he said.

"Watch me?"

My eyes ached and I reached up to rub them with the back of my free hand. "Watch me?" I mumbled. "Creepy."

"Gawain said you'd say that," Henry sighed a small huff of laughter. "For that very reason he said he hoped he wasn't on duty when you woke up."

"Gawain..." I muttered. My brain felt muddy. I knew something...

Reaching into my pocket, I made sure I still had the MP3 player. It survived whatever the hell I had gone through and I set it on the floor beside my bed. "Still safe," I muttered.

"And you?" Henry asked. "Are you safe?"

"Yeah..." I yawned. "Why wouldn't I be?"

Henry frowned deeply. "Socorro, you were missing for two days and you've been asleep here in bed for three."

"The fuck?" I went to sit up again and paused.

"Easy Rip Van Winkle." He stood and put his arm behind my shoulders to help me sit up. That worry was still there in his eyes, entirely genuine.

Why would he even care?

"Can you tell me what happened?" he asked as he retook his seat.

I closed my left eye and squinted, trying to remember. I had walked through a dream and trying to recall the events felt like my blanket grew warmer and heavier. The more I tried to think back on it, the more it lulled and settled, pressing comfortingly over me like a hug from my mother. My eyes fluttered. I breathed deeply and my head tipped forward until my chin tapped my chest. The memories weren't coming to me, only the ease of slumber.

"Socorro?"

Henry's voice cut through the fog and in the dark behind my eyelids, I remembered them. I remembered Galahad and the knights. I remembered Mordred... and the way his dark eyes stared back at me through time.

"Galahad," I said to Henry and the word came out croaked and dry. "I was following Galahad."

He sat up a little straighter and folded his hands in his lap. "What... do you mean you were *following* Galahad?" he asked. "Like... a feeling? Like—"

"Like I saw him walking through the woods and I followed him," I replied. "He was on patrol with Sir Gawain and Sir Perceval. They're... a bit older than him."

"Patrol?" Henry stared at me.

Did knights not go on patrol? I was beginning to second guess myself. Maybe I was only imagining things. I was out there for a few days. What if I had been dehydrated and dying and my brain made things up?

"They were hunting Lancelot and Princess Iona... They seemed to think they were on their way to the Black Spire?" I put my face in my hands. "This sounds like nonsense," I whined.

"Not nonsense," Henry shook his head quickly. "What else?"

I groaned and dropped my head all the way back to stare at the ceiling. "I don't know! Mordred showed up?"

"M—" The word wouldn't form on his lips. He looked like he was about to choke.

I sighed, "Please tell me this isn't one of those 'He-who-shall-not-be-named' types of people."

"No," Henry once again shook his head. "Mordred is... You followed Sir Galahad?"

Mordred was what? I wanted to talk about him. He was…
Well, I didn't know what he was but I had so many
questions. Too many.

"I followed him," I confirmed instead. "And then I was
him. And…"

I felt my frustration rising. Henry had said that the heirs
weren't reincarnations but he never said that we weren't
vessels or something for their spirits. I swallowed hard and
my hands gripped each other in my lap. My thoughts ran
away from me. They had all told me that we were not at the
direct mercy of our predecessors, only the expectations that
we succeed as their descendants.

What if that was different for me? There was absolutely no
reason for me to be different or special in my life. Henry was
practically a prince of a long gone, nearly mythical kingdom.
Why wasn't he the special one? Sure, they kept calling me *a*
grail knight but not *the* grail knight. There was more than
just one.

"This… this doesn't happen to you, does it?" I hesitated to
ask.

"No."

I appreciated the honesty. I hated the confirmation.

Henry stood and went to the window. His hands clasped
behind his back and his expression became solemn in the
orange light of the waning sun. "I am descended of Arthur,"
he said, "but the king still lives. I don't get passing… deja vu
the way everyone else does. I get… feelings. I don't believe
they are the king's."

"Queen Guinevere?" I asked and he nodded.

"Merlin assures me I am the heir of Arthur and Guinevere,
but I…"

He had doubts. What if he wasn't King Arthur's heir? Did

he think he didn't belong here? The descendant of the fabled adulterous queen.

"Mordred tried to take Camelot once," he said, "when Arthur was on campaign. Our history is... muddy at that time."

"I know how Galahad felt about Mordred," I said to Henry.

Galahad saw Mordred as an irredeemable traitor, not just to the kingdom but to himself. Whatever Mordred had done, it had destroyed any ties between them and Galahad wished him dead. Mordred very well could have assaulted the queen when he usurped the throne. Men were capable of terrible things, but something wiggled in the quiet part of my brain with certainty. Mordred was more than capable of terrible things, but never that.

"If you were the heir of Mordred and Queen Guinevere, I do not think you would be here," I said after a moment.

Henry flashed that million-dollar smile back at me. There was humor in his face, relaxation in his shoulders. I had said something that calmed his troubled mind. "You sound different," he told me.

My face scrunched. What did he mean by that?

"Something about your... I don't know, word choice? It's different," he said. "You and you almost sound like you actually want to be here."

"Go fuck yourself, Henry," I scoffed.

He laughed, "Nevermind then."

I laughed and my muscles ached. I groaned and leaned back against the headboard with a *thump*.

Henry turned his back to the window and set his hands beside him on the sill. The afternoon sun turned him into a silhouette and I couldn't see his expression anymore. It was ominous and if he was going for an effect, he was succeeding.

"I don't get guidance from King Arthur..." he thought aloud.

"Could be because he's not dead," I offered.

"And you can step into Galahad's past as if you're living his memories."

"Yeah..." I nodded and decided to tell him a little more. "I'm pretty sure he's talking to me in my head, too."

"...What?"

I told him. The push to the castle ruins. Arguing over Merlin's wishes. I was certain those were him, and I was almost positive it was Galahad that encouraged me to run from my father that night he and Eddel found me.

Henry stood very still. Silence settled between us for a moment until he abruptly broke it with, "Bullshit."

I snorted and held my chest at the ache that followed. Hearing him cuss was kind of funny. "You don't believe me?"

He crossed his arms and sat on the window sill. He was restless, shifting one leg and then the other. His hands slid down his body to rest on his knees and his head bowed as he stared down at the floor.

"Henry?" my voice trembled. "You're really starting to freak me out."

"Sir Galahad prayed before the grail for a year," he said as if reciting from a dry manuscript. "He prayed to God for death, to ascend to heaven."

"So what does that mean, Henry? He didn't really die?" My voice raised in a mixture of fear and anger. "What does that *mean*?"

"I don't know!" he shot back, raising his hands and clenching and unclenching them in the air before he gripped the back of his neck. "He's dead. Galahad died. I was told that Galahad died, just not like everyone else."

"How the fuck do you die differently than everyone else?"

His shoulders drew up. He held out his empty hands towards me as he shrugged. I couldn't see his face but I could tell his jaw was open without an ideas of how to answer my question. He made a wordless sound like *buh* and finally told me, "Sir Perceval returned with the account but it was vague, little more than a poem."

I drew a long deep breath and held it. My ancestor wasn't dead. Not *dead* dead. Not like everyone else's. Did I have to deal with a dead knight playing push and pull with the rest of my life?

Exhaling all of the air in my lungs, my words came out in a breathy rush as I asked, "Can he come back?"

"I don't know, Sox."

The lack of formality made me feel a little better. Had anyone outside of the heirs called me that, I would have been livid. The familiarity was reassuring, as if we had always been friends.

"I'll ask Merlin," he said as he slapped his knees before standing.

"No!" my voice was louder than intended and he froze halfway up from the window sill. "No... just... I know this is something that Merlin should know... but I just got here Henry. Today was my first lesson and it wasn't even good. If I wake up after being unconscious and become a case study...?"

Henry nodded. He understood what I was trying to say and returned to the chair at my bedside. Reaching over, he set his hand on mine again and gave it a squeeze. "Alright," he said. "We keep this all to ourselves for now unless the voices, the jumps to the past, the disappearing acts get worse."

I set my other hand on top of his and nodded. "Okay."

"Okay."

"But uh… It's just one voice and a lot of weird vibes."

Henry nodded slowly as if he were agreeing with a child. "If the vibes get weirder, we're telling Merlin."

Amicable quiet settled between us and I found myself staring out the window as the oranges began to blue with dusk.

"You're the heir of Galahad," Henry said and I heard humor in his voice. "I'm interested to see how you handle a sword."

"I'm gonna lose a finger," I grumbled.

Henry stayed with me a bit longer, helping me get back on my feet and out to the table where Eddel brought us dinner. She was relieved that I was vertical again. That meant they no longer had to take shifts to watch over me.

"Merlin said that your body isn't used to the magic," Eddel told me. "It's overwhelming your senses now that you're here."

Something certainly was. Whether it was just the magic or the pushy presence that had infiltrated my brain, or both, I didn't really know. Henry and I kept our secret. We didn't mention Galahad to Eddel and we wouldn't unless things got worse.

"You're fairly scrawny," Henry mused between bites of warm potato soup.

"Gee, thanks," I grumbled back. I felt like I could barely stomach any food. My body was heavy and repeatedly lifting my spoon was draining.

"I meant," Henry sighed, "perhaps if you become stronger

in body and in mind, you won't... black out anymore."

He meant: I wouldn't get pushed around by the voices in my head anymore. This was a strange place and the logic was sound as far as I knew.

"You're really going to have to buckle down in your lessons then," Eddel said and patted my shoulder as she passed me to retrieve a water pitcher and refill my cup. "But you should really be giving them your all anyway."

I resisted the urge to reply: *yes mother*.

I felt recovered enough the next morning to rejoin Valeria again in the practice circle. She insisted we take it slow and I wasn't about to argue. I needed slow anyway. I didn't know what I was doing. Valeria didn't ask me what had happened or how or why I had gone missing. I assumed she had been filled in by someone else. The only public response I had given was that I didn't remember anything at all. There was no reason for them not to believe me, and there wasn't any indication that they didn't.

My sword lessons took place between breakfast and lunch, and in between lunch and dinner I had riding lessons at the barn. Cars existed in the outside world, but in the sanctuary, everyone knew how to ride a horse and Gawain's mother Saoirse was the resident horsemaster. On my first day, she gave me a demonstration of the things she would be teaching me. I didn't know it was possible for a person to swing off the side of a horse and pluck a flower from the ground at a gallop. I doubted that would be a party trick I would pick up any time soon, or even with years of practice.

"You should know," she told me, "that is almost impossible for me to do in armor." She rubbed her shoulder. Something told me she had hit the ground plenty enough times trying to figure it out how to keep her balance and reach for the ground.

As it turned out, I was terrified of horses, but Saoirse was as kind in personality as she appeared. She was patient and never rushed me. She started me mucking stalls and grooming. Becoming more confident with a sword seemed to bring me confidence everywhere else.

Within a few short weeks I was finally on a horse. Though I immediately came off the other side with a graceless yelp.

"Holding Out for a Hero!" Gawain had called out from the fence of the corral. "Bonnie Tyler."

The impact knocked the wind out of me and I couldn't clamber back to my feet as fast as I wanted to. I managed an impolite middle finger and he howled with laughter as he continued on his way.

I never believed in coincidence. The stables were behind the village and further away from the rest of the training areas. I doubted he had made an unscheduled appearance. Either way, he left in good humor as I dusted myself off, but he was never out of sight for very long.

There were days here and there that the village seemed quieter, days when my lesson schedule changed. When Valeria was gone for a week, I learned the history of Albion with Merlin and had horse lessons in the evening. When Gawain's mother Saoirse was gone for several days along with Valeria, I had lessons with Merlin in the morning, and in the afternoons, very awkward dance lessons with Gabriel's father Lucas.

"I hope you don't fight or ride a horse like this," Lucas laughed at me as I stumbled through a waltz with him at arms length.

I grumbled, "I can do those on my own without touching anybody."

"You mainland *americanos* with your distrust of physical intimacy," he said, making *physical intimacy* sound like something spooky and haunting. "You act like a *gringo*."

"A gri—!" I huffed, "Puerto Rico is part of the U.S.!

"I refuse."

I didn't think that was a thing that a person could refuse. But I really didn't know enough about colonization at that time to know any better.

A few lessons passed before I felt like I could trust Lucas enough to really lead me in a dance. Once more, he was patient, never rushing. He always spoke to me as an equal. All of my instructors did, except Merlin, whom at least treated me like an adult. I knew I didn't have all of the time in the world to learn what should have been taught to me my entire life, but they were trying, and so was I.

Eventually, I started having fun on the dance floor. I could look Lucas in the eye and remember the steps while still holding a conversation. There were so many dances to remember and each one seemed to build upon the other. Dancing was as easy as swordplay, which wasn't very easy at all. I was by no means a master in anything, but they had all assured me that I was making admirable progress and had a good handle of the basics. I could feel it in myself, in the ways I became more flexible, in the new ways my body ached.

When my lessons with Merlin finally branched into court etiquette, he told me, "Humor me," before we even started. He knew me too well by then. I had to humor him, and even myself. Etiquette, in all of its forms, wasn't exactly something I cared about. Even dancing was better than that.

Days blended together like some kind of movie montage. I had arrived in our sanctuary village in March. By the end of

April, my training was hardly complete but the chicken-armed girl had turned her entire life around. I ate, slept, and drank my lessons. I had nothing else to do but train and learn while the sun was still in the sky. I hadn't been one for making and maintaining new friendships before, and even Gawain and Henry had fallen to the back burner. I lived with Eddel and barely saw her outside of a few minutes in the morning and a few minutes in the evening. I was constantly running to the next thing, or too tired to talk before I went to sleep at night.

At the end of my training montage, Merlin finally threw his hands in the air and said, "I need you to leave for a few days."

"What?" I stared at him as I stood on the threshold of our classroom. "Leave?"

"You have been a model student, but you have spent no time with your comrades, nor your family."

"I thought that was what you wanted...?" I muttered.

"A model student, yes," he sighed. "More informed about your history? Also yes. But I simply cannot keep up with your demands. Valeria is exhausted. Saoirse is stuck trying to find a way to keep you from getting bored in your lessons. You haven't stepped on Lucas's feet in weeks! You can't keep pushing yourself like this—"

"I feel fine!" I complained.

"Fine," he snorted. "Then we can't keep pushing ourselves like this. Take a break so that we can as well."

I stared at him.

"You heard me," said the sorcerer and he pointed at the door. "Go."

"Where?"

"Somewhere!" he said. "Anywhere!"

"Fine!" I shouted.

I slammed the door as I walked back out and found I had drawn the attention of my father's sword class.

"You alright there?" Quinn asked. I knew his face a little better after stealing his mother for over a month. We weren't friends, but we weren't strangers. He had his mother's eyes: friendly and so dark that they were almost black. Many people were always put off by such color. It made his face even more striking, handsome almost. Or rather, Quinn would be handsome if he didn't share his mother's signature scowl.

"Merlin's kicking me out for a bit," I sighed.

My father walked toward Quinn, his short sword raised to swat him the way I had once seen him do to Gawain. Without even looking, Quinn raised his sword and blocked the attack with a swish of his wrist.

"Good," Quinn told me as if he were merely swatting a fly that happened to be shaped like my father. "Go do something so I can have my mother back for a while."

I smiled sheepishly and looked to Gawain. Did he feel the same way about me stealing his mother for lessons? Did Gabriel when I took his father Lucas? That was selfish of me. Just because I didn't want to hang out with my father didn't mean they didn't want to spend time with their parents.

"Back to work," my father announced.

The class shifted where they stood, though no one really seemed to be listening to him. All eyes were on me and I felt that gnawing sense of uncertainty creep up my spine. I thought it was gone, replaced by knowledge and capability. Some things simply didn't change, no matter how much confidence was built around it. If the problem wasn't solved, the trouble would persist. Anxiety, however, wasn't exactly a solvable problem.

Their attention made me feel unwanted and I hurriedly made my departure. I trotted off toward Eddel's home and somehow found myself running. Running was... fun. I enjoyed it. I didn't think of it as an escape, more like I was running *to* something. With my lessons grinding to a halt early in the day, I had more energy than I knew what to do with. Perhaps I had exhausted my instructors after all. They hadn't had to work so hard before with students that came in with some kind of background, some kind of balance.

Crossing the threshold into Eddel's home, I found her sitting at the table with Nancy. "Back already?" she asked me.

Nancy dropped her gaze to the table. I hadn't really spoken with Nancy before. I knew of her by name and in passing. Her short dark hair hung straight down to her shoulders and I watched her shyly push the strands behind her ear, a nervous gesture. She wouldn't look at me. Nancy was the heir of Lancelot and Queen Guinevere when both had been bewitched through means that had not yet been clarified to me, though I suspected Mordred had a hand in it. I wondered if that suspicion was from something I knew, or something that Galahad knew. Though, he had said something to that effect when I had stepped into his memories.

"Merlin wants me to take time off," I shrugged as I turned and went for my room.

"Time off?" Eddel said.

If she continued, I hadn't heard her. The last several weeks I hadn't listened to her at all, or had given her partial answers because my mind was everywhere else but in the moment with her.

Pausing in step at the threshold of my room, I braced my hands on the door frame. I had time again, and I had energy. A thought crossed my mind and I glanced back to the two of them. "How many heirs are girls?" I asked.

"Five total," Eddel said and I stared at her. She looked at me quizzically. "What?"

"There's seventy some-odd heirs and there's only five girls?"

"It's what happens when there are offspring of an unapproved match." Eddel told me. "All of the heirs were supposed to be male."

Valeria had mentioned that. I had yelled at Merlin about that.

"Okay okay," I shook my head. "So you, me, Nancy? Then the redhead with the accent and the other girl? The Indian girl."

"Chandra," Eddel told me with a hint of disapproval and shook her head.

"You still don't know everyone's names?" Nancy gawked. There was a little bit of an accent to her words. French, perhaps?

"I'm an unsocialized dog," I commented easily. It wasn't a lie. That was a recurring comment that seemed to spread up in the elders of the village. Lucas had told me as much during one of my dance lessons.

"They have little respect for you," he had said. "They think you don't belong here."

"I don't," I told him.

He spun me and when we met again, he said, "Never say that, Socorro. You belong here. Even if you aren't what they want you to be. Be what you know you are."

"An asshole?" I asked.

114

"An asshole," he agreed with a chuckle.

A smile edged at the corners of Nancy's mouth and it quickly went away. She was somewhat humored with my self-degradation. I was glad I wasn't the only one.

"Lilias is the redhead," Eddel informed me.

"Alright, there's five of us, that's not so big a number," I said and tapped my fingers on the wooden door frame. "I have an idea!"

"Okay...?" Eddel said slowly.

"Girls' night," I grinned.

"Girls' night?" they echoed.

"Yeah. We need a united front against all the dopes out there. Might as well get to know one another, have some fun, play some games, watch some movies. Cause some mischief." I was encouraging shenanigans, and also, I wanted a chance to make up for my behavior toward Eddel. I was in her home and I was a neglectful house guest. I was sailing down the river of bad friendship and I didn't want to do that.

Eddel appeared stricken. She looked pale, which was surprising to see when her skin was so very dark. "I... I've never left the village."

"All the better reason to go," I said. "I'll be with you."

"Is the new Marvel movie out?" Nancy asked and slowly raised her attention to me. Her eyes were hazel, similar to they way mine looked when I last saw them in the mirror of my bathroom. Was that a trait of the heirs of Lancelot? Did the redhead Lilias also have hazel eyes?

"Black Panther came out in February," I said.

"Aw, I missed it," Nancy grumbled.

"I'm pretty sure it's going to be in theaters for a while," I assured her. It was still breaking box office numbers when I had left and had shown no sign of slowing down.

"I haven't been to the movies in ages," Nancy whispered to herself.

"I've... never been?" Eddel said and the room grew quiet. When she said she hadn't left the village, she had meant it. She had grown up here. She had seen movies, just not in the theater. She knew a few references, but I wondered if she knew where they were from or if they had simply been explained to her over the years.

"Then we should go," I said.

"I don't know..." Eddel muttered. She seemed a little smaller where she sat at the table. I didn't know she was capable of even appearing vulnerable. It didn't look right on her. Eddel wasn't just the first to arrive in the village, the leader of us all, and the heir of the original grail knight Sir Perceval. She was a young woman who could still dislike change and uncertainty as much as the rest of us.

Merlin still hadn't told me what it meant to be a grail knight. He changed the subject every time I asked. What he had told me, however, was that it would be up to Eddel and me. That it was in our blood. His ranting became confusing after that and I forced him to change the subject rather than sit through another agonizing, headache inducing lecture.

"I'll be right there with you the whole time," I assured Eddel.

A gentle smile crossed her face. She wasn't wholly convinced, but she seemed a little more accepting when she knew she wasn't going to be alone in the wild world outside. "Okay," she finally agreed.

Eddel was certainly in for a culture shock.

"I'm in," Nancy agreed with more enthusiasm than I had ever seen come from her, even if it was little more than a

116

quick nod of her head. She seemed excited, though. And she let her excitement stay on the surface, not as quick to pack it away and hide.

"Then we just need to talk to Lilias and Chandra," I said. "Aaaand... I don't know them."

"I'll get Lil," Nancy replied.

"I've got Chandra," Eddel said and they were on their feet and out the door.

I smiled to myself and went to pack a bag. A few things had made their way from home through Merlin: more clothes, a few razors that I still hadn't used, sanitary pads that were almost completely gone, and my soft blue microfleece blanket. My favorite blanket. It really helped make my room at Eddel's place feel livable. There were pictures on my dresser of my mother and me, a figurine from one of my favorite games, and beside that was two bunched up crusty socks and the little folded piece of paper from Gawain that I had never read.

So many days had passed since that night I had left my father's house and moved in with Eddel. I didn't think of that night often, and when it did come to mind, I didn't remember him. I remembered Henry and Eddel. I saw their commanding figures protecting me. King Arthur and Sir Perceval, my friends.

The sleepover was a good idea. I thought it was best I know the other three women, even if it was a bit late after my arrival. Two of them were heirs of Lancelot like myself, which had to mean something. Chandra, from what I had heard, was the heir of Sir Kay, the close confidant and companion of the last knight to see Excalibur, Sir Bedivere.

One thing Merlin had taught me was that events seldom happened among us without reason. Did I want to believe that some secret thing would happen with all five female heirs together? No. Did I think it was possible? More than anything. Did I hope it would simply be a weird bonding moment? Yes. I really did.

CHAPTER EIGHT

Sleepover

Merlin appeared on the verge of a heart attack when I told him the five of us were leaving. "Together?" he squawked as if it were a bad thing.

I had gotten too used to the old sorcerer and I brazenly replied, "Yup. And you're not stopping us. We're working on that whole camaraderie thing. Maybe it'll help me feel like this is my home."

He glared at me. Merlin wasn't stupid. I was using his own words against him. He wanted nothing more than for all of us to get along and figure it out, but when he gave his approval for us to go, there was something in his eyes that made me uneasy.

Either way, I didn't hesitate to get us the hell out of there. I slapped that stone pillar, opened the portal and rushed us through it before he could change his mind.

My house was quiet except for my mom sitting on the couch watching television. She looked up when we came in and leapt to her feet. "*Mija!*" she cried out and ran to me.

Her arms wrapped around me and she squeezed me until I thought I would fart, or worse. "Maaaa," I whined and she let me go when she noticed the other four behind me.

"You brought friends!" she said excitedly and hugged me again.

The girls giggled. It was obvious I didn't really bring people home. I actively avoided it. I went to other people's houses when I was in school. I didn't want anyone running the risk of meeting my father. I didn't like the risk of running into him either.

I spun around in my mother's grip and introduced them. My mother still hadn't let me go, but she held on with one hand, her chin on my shoulder, as she reached around me to shake their hands.

"We're here for a few days," I said. "Merlin kicked me out."

"Already?" my mother balked.

"Just for a few days," I assured her.

"I will make food! You girls are hungry, right? Of course. I could eat too!" My mother finally flew away from me and into the kitchen. I glanced around the house, it was spotless. She had moved things around, had repainted the walls, had hung pictures of the two of us. There was no sign that my father ever lived here at all.

"What have you been up to?" I called as I heard the refrigerator open and close.

"Amelia, Henry's mother, flew in for a few weeks and helped me get everything squared away with the house," my mother called back. "She's an amazing woman. And Sebastián, Quinn's father, is expanding his business stateside and asked me to join his team, so I have been keeping busy."

Merlin hadn't lied. Those left behind took care of one another. I grinned broadly and couldn't hide it as I rounded the corner to peek into the kitchen. Spotless. She had refinished the cabinets and they were painted white with little blue flowers on the doors. Everything was vibrant and refreshed. She looked happy. The house looked happy without *him*.

"Please tell me you didn't touch my room," I muttered.

"Oh no, that's yours. It's still as messy as you left it," she said.

There was a pause after her words and I could almost feel my fellow heirs shift where they stood. Before I could stop them, they were tore down the hallway opening doors in an effort to catch my troubled room before I was able to clean it.

"Goddamnit," I sighed and trudged after them to the sound of my mother's laughing. She had done that on purpose. Of course she did. I knew where I got my attitude from, even if she denied it.

"Whoa," echoed down the hall.

"It's not that bad!" I exclaimed.

When I got to the door, I realized they weren't shocked, but in awe of the movie posters on the walls and on the ceiling. I flipped on the light and the fan started up with a gentle sway. It was a little rickety. I had never minded, the tapping rocked me to sleep on restless nights.

There were game consoles on the tall dresser and low shelves around the room filled with books. One full wall had my world map. I had plans to mark off the places I visited one day. So far, it was entirely blank. The only piece of land that I could mark existed in some magical dimension, ripped straight out of Albion and protected since the fall of King Arthur.

"Your room at home is so small compared to this," Eddel said. Home. She called the village our home and I wanted to say that it wasn't. The words didn't come out. Though, this wasn't exactly my home either. Not anymore. I was in

121

between, straddling the portal with no real place of my own.

"Ah ne'er wid hae guessed ye were yin of us," Lilias said, her accent thick in her mouth, though she seemed to have slowed it down for my benefit. I had heard her talking to Nancy a time or two in passing. I never would have understood her, and I imagined that sometimes Nancy didn't either. Smile and nod.

Lilias was a true redhead, and a very Scottish redhead at that. I would need to keep her out of the Texas sun while she visited. Even in late April it was possible to burn, and she was so pale I imagined she would sizzle to a crisp without supervision.

"Why not?" I asked.

"Even I had knights and horses somewhere in my room," Eddel said as she looked around at my walls.

"I had swords in my room," Nancy told me.

Chandra, quiet and reserved since the moment we were first introduced, dropped to sit on the corner of my bed and sighed, "I had shields decorating my walls."

Chandra was gorgeous. I didn't know much about Indian cultures or dress outside of the few Bollywood movies I had seen. Shah Rukh Khan and Aishwarya Rai were two of my favorite actors, stateside and international, but it didn't mean I knew anything about India as a whole. What I did know about Chandra was that she—for as reserved as she looked—had an engine of a mind. I could see it in her eyes, the way she observed every little thing about me and my room. When she was deepest in thought, she pulled her obscenely long braided hair over her shoulder and ran her fingers over the twists. She always seemed to dress fairly westernized—today was no different—but with her own cultural flair. The bright colors, the saree, the patterns.

I wished I had some kind of culture of my own. I didn't. I was stuck in between White America and Pick-And-Choose Mexican-American, who had to be more American than every other American to try and fit in. I had never celebrated *Dia de los Muertos*, *Dia de los Reyes Magos*, *Semana Santa*. Not even *Carnaval*! My mother had talked about these things at least once or twice when I was growing up. Within the past few years, we barely celebrated Christmas anymore.

"Um…" I looked around at all of them. "Did you guys get to pick anything that went in your rooms?"

They were silent again. They were raised knowing their history. They were molded, nicely trimmed topiaries. I was a tangled mass of nettles.

"So," I said slowly when it seemed none of them were going to talk. "I think I have a movie you guys are going to love."

Not sure what made me think Monty Python and the Holy Grail was the best choice, but the horrified humor on their faces was the best thing I had ever seen. Four young women sat around my room laughing so hard during the film that at one point, Nancy cried out, "I'm going to pee myself!"

"Not on my bed!" I shot back. They only laughed harder.

I had seen this movie more times than I could count, but with them I watched it completely anew. I had more knowledge, about ourselves, about Albion. The jokes were twice as funny and with the others there, it was even more so. Perhaps it was because we saw ourselves in the places of these characters of whom we were supposed to be the heirs of. Or maybe it was because everything I had been taught was intense and solemn. It was life and death, hope and treason, victory and defeat. And this was absurd and lighthearted. I welcomed it after everything I had learned.

"Did he pronounce it Ga-*lee*-had?" Nancy asked during the movie.

The girls laughed. I felt my face become a little warm. I was going to become Galeehad. I just knew it…

My mother brought us food and she sat with me for a while, leaning her head on my shoulder. She was happy to have me home. She looked at the others and said, "They're enjoying themselves," as she ran her fingers over the pendants on her necklace.

She had worn that necklace for as long as I could remember. One was a dainty little golden cross, and the other a circle with a rectangle inside of it. I asked her once what the circle was and she always shrugged. An heirloom passed down from her mother. She had patted my head and told me one day she would pass it on to me. I was old enough to tell her no thanks. Heirloom or not, I wasn't one for shiny jewelry.

I was glad my mother could tell that my fellow heirs were having fun. Even Chandra's reserved demeanor had fallen away. After dinner, it was snacks and more movies, a few of my mother's favorites like Cat Ballou and Leap Year. And then a few of my own guilty pleasures like Pacific Rim and Better Off Dead. I loved John Cusack movies.

One by one they started drifting off to sleep as the sky outside began to turn pale into the next morning. A mass of bodies laid side by side on my bed and I stretched out across the foot of my bed and joined them. I tucked my arms beneath my head and stared up at the poster-covered ceiling. It didn't take long for the tapping of the fan lulled me to sleep.

I discovered the next afternoon that my mother had called in to work to stay home with us. Quinn's father was more than accommodating. After all, how often did the heirs return home to visit? And en masse? I had learned that phrase from Nancy. She was French.

We awoke slowly at different times. When I wandered from my room, Lilias was taking a shower and Eddel was having a late lunch with my mother at the table. They spoke of home, whatever home was for them. My mother missed Mexico, but she wasn't going to leave. I was here, for the most part. Eddel spoke of a place she couldn't quite remember, a place that she wasn't sure if it was memory or imagination. She longed for it, wherever it was.

As I opened the fridge, I heard Eddel say, "Merlin raised me. If there's anything he knows of my parents, he refuses to say."

I had been correct in seeing some kind of similarity between the two of them. Merlin had raised her, and Eddel had taken on some mannerisms. I wondered if I pushed her too far the way I had Merlin, if she too would kick me out for a few days.

"Don't leave the fridge open like that," my mother said and I grabbed the milk and closed the door.

Cereal. She still kept the colorful junk with the marshmallows for me. We didn't have much food before, and with me out of the house the pantry was full. The marshmallow cereal was a treat for those really bad days. This wasn't a bad day. I decided it would be a celebratory cereal instead and I poured myself a bowl and sat beside my mother at the table.

"Nancy and Chandra are still out," I said.

"Who is the heir of who?" my mother asked.

"Perceval," Eddel said as she raised her hand a little.

"Galahad," I said. "Lilias, the redhead, is Lancelot and

Princess Iona. Nancy is Lancelot and Queen Guinevere, and Chandra is Sir Kay."

"Sir Kay? The companion of Bedivere? Oh I loved Sir Bedivere's stories," my mother sighed appreciatively. "He was a witch, you know."

"A what?" Eddel stared at her.

I glared at my mother. "What about Galahad?" I muttered.

She made a face as she said, "Oh, he's not a witch."

"Mom!"

"I'm not saying anything," she told me, "You'll get offended."

"I won't!"

"He was a stuffy goody-goody."

I stared at her. Eddel's face paled. I imagined no one spoke about the Knights of the Round Table in this way.

"Sounds right," I shrugged. It did. What kind of devotion did a person need to pray for death for a year straight? That was a boredom I wanted no part of.

"So..." my mother said and leaned forward. She looked to Eddel and then to me and nudged my arm. "Are there any cute boys in this village of yours?"

Simultaneously, Eddel and I replied, "I haven't noticed."

We looked at each other.

"We're not exactly allowed or encouraged to think that way," I clarified to my mother. "Merlin doesn't want the bloodlines mixing, or something like that."

"Ohhhhh," she said and nodded. "I didn't know. That's..." She interrupted herself with a shake of her head and complained, "What, are you expected to be nuns?"

Eddel laughed.

"I think, we're supposed to wait," I said between spoonfuls of cereal.

126

My mother's nose wrinkled. "Abstinence education doesn't work," she said and then glanced to me before telling Eddel, "Believe me I know."

"Mom!" I squawked.

"It's… how we're raised," Eddel told her. "Many of the heirs, myself included, are brought up on the idea of chastity, including the men. Pure and pious."

"I'll never get grandchildren," my mother sighed.

"That's it, I'm going to go eat my cereal outside where it's less awkward," I said and rose to my feet.

"It's two in the afternoon," my mother said, "It's not very sunny but it's still eighty degrees and the clouds are rolling in. If it rains, the mosquitoes will eat you."

I paused as I stared out the sliding glass door behind her. She was right. I had become too accustomed to the mild weather of our village and the pleasant lack of bloodsucking insects. Eighty something degrees was definitely hot. I didn't want to be here during summer.

"That is a problem…" I muttered to myself as I bit the corner of my lip and frowned.

My mother whispered something to Eddel and I distracted mumbled, "What?"

"She asked if you were sick," Eddel told me.

"Sick?"

"You're just so…" My mother seemed to be searching for the word somewhere in the air around her head and finally settled with, "chill."

I blinked a few times and grumbled, "Yeah, fair enough."

"See!" my mother cried. "What is this?"

I rolled my eyes and sighed.

Lilias and Chandra entered the dining room then and I pointed to the refrigerator and said, "Foods in there. Make yourselves at home. Mom's bad at breakfast."

"I am not!" my mother huffed.

"Says the woman that gave me half an eggshell in my breakfast taco."

"One time!" she shot back.

"Six. Stop cooking eggs. You're a nuisance to society," I told her and then stepped quickly out of reach as she swiped at me.

"Oooh, I take it back, you haven't changed a bit!" she scoffed.

I smiled and continued eating my cereal as I walked around the table to stand by Eddel. "Love you too," I told my mother. She smiled at me.

While the others dug into their own breakfast, Nancy finally joined us, and I begged my mother once again not to try and cook anything for us that involved breakfast foods. She did anyway, and much to the amusement of everyone, I still bit right into a piece of eggshell. I had been the guinea pig.

They laughed. I shouted, "I told you!" and held it out to her.

My mother said, "I did it on purpose!"

"Villain!" I cried. That only made them laugh even worse.

No one ate their eggs except Eddel—who was much too nice—but the bacon disappeared.

I didn't for a second believe that my mother accosted me with eggshells on purpose. I imagined she was trying her best, her face had showed her determination. It simply wasn't enough. If I wanted migas, I had to do it myself, or at least crack the eggs for her.

"I was thinking," I mused as we all sat around the table. "Mom, could you drop us off at the mall?"

She looked around the at all of us and said, "None of you have a driver's license?"

"Why would we?" I asked. "We live on a magical island with no cars and a grouchy all-knowing sorcerer as our warden."

"It's not an island," Chandra corrected.

"Ah wonder how faur it goes," Lilias said and tapped her chin. "Whit're the boundaries?"

"That's something to investigate," I muttered.

"We probably shouldn't," Nancy said, her gaze downcast the way I had seen her in Eddel's home.

I shrugged and told her, "Eh, just blame it on me. Merlin's used to me causing trouble by now. If we get into it, point at me and say I made you do it."

"I like that idea," Eddel said.

Glancing to her as she sat smiling at my right, I said, "Eddel... I mean in this one instance. If we're all caught together exploring the non-island. Don't go blaming me for every little thing."

"Oh no," Eddel told me with an even broader grin. "Only the worst of things."

"Rude," I muttered.

Nancy chuckled.

"So!" I quickly corrected us back to my original question. "Mall?" I asked my mother.

"I can. What do I get out of it?" my mother asked.

"You can get me not asking for money for useless crap since we're just going to wander around aimlessly like weird high school kids with nothing better to do."

My mother looked around the table at us and then said, "None of you have money, do you?"

"We live on a magical island," Eddel said and the smiles

grew on the faces of the others.

"Oh, it's okay when she says it's an island?" I balked.

"Eddel has seniority," Chandra chuckled.

I made a face. I was the last one to show up, but I still didn't expect that to matter. Boy was I wrong. I grumbled, "Alright, alright."

"Eddel is going to get culture shock," Nancy said.

"Probably," Eddel agreed. "I can't remember living in this world. This is a first for me."

"You're handling it admirably," my mother assured her.

Eddel was an amazing woman. I had seen her handle a sword. She was flawless in her form, terrific on horse, with a bow, with patience. She was a master of the knight's Code of Chivalry. She was the closest to becoming a knight of any of us and I counted her among my friends. Eddel, however, could not handle rush hour traffic in San Antonio, Texas. It wasn't even one of the bigger cities, but it probably didn't help that it was storming pretty hard. San Antonio had occasional trouble, but it wasn't at all like Houston or Dallas.

The ungodly screech that came from Eddel's mouth almost made me wet myself while laughing.

"What was that?" Nancy gawked.

"Di' we skelp something?" Lilias asked and rolled down the window to look out as we passed beneath a bridge. Eddel yanked her back in.

I was glad I was sitting in the front passenger seat and none of them could see my face as I doubled over and covered my mouth to hold back whatever awful laugh was about to escape my soul. I desperately tried to keep this from triggering some kind of ugly, uncontrollable demon-cackle.

My mother dropped us at the covered entrance to the mall and said, "Call me when you're ready." Then she dug into her purse and held out a folded wad of cash. "Here. Have fun."

"Mom...?" I didn't reach for it. We hadn't ever had money before. I was fully intending to do nothing but hang out and walk around stores. I had even said as much before she brought us. "Are you sure?"

"We're not hurting anymore, *mija*," she told me with a smile. "Have fun. Don't kill Eddel."

"I mean... are you really sure?" I tried to confirm.

"Socorro," she said. "Don't kill Eddel."

"No, I mean—"

"Take the damn money," she took my hand and stuffed it in my palm. If I'd tried to refuse, she might have thrown it at me.

She waved at us from the car, told us once more to have fun, and drove away.

"I see where you get it from," Eddel grinned.

I rounded on Eddel with a smart comment on the tip of my tongue, but Nancy spoke first.

"Money issues?" she asked.

"Yeah," I said and pocketed the cash. "We were dead broke when I left. Dad didn't do shit. Mom legally couldn't get a job because they weren't married and she isn't a citizen. If it weren't for Quinn's dad, I guess there's no telling what would have happened to her... I'll have to thank him."

"My dad died when I was young," Nancy said. There was no hesitation. She said it outright and she didn't even flinch. I couldn't even tell if it bothered her. "He was the blood-bearer. My mom raised me and we were the same as you, barely scraping by. The day I turned eighteen, Merlin came for me and after I left, she started getting help from the other parents, too."

That was odd. Why wait to help us until we left. Was it a payment? A trade? Being poor didn't build character, it built contempt. I wanted to say this aloud. I wanted their input. It made me angry and it wasn't the first time I had thought about this.

"How's your mom, now?" I asked instead. Contrary to popular belief, I did know how to watch my mouth. Usually, I just chose not to.

Nancy shoved her hands deep into her pockets and said, "Haven't seen her in about a year. She dropped away from the others after getting on her feet. Remarried last year and has a new family now."

"Fuck..." Lilias and I breathed.

Chandra frowned. "I'm sorry, Nancy, I didn't know."

Nancy shrugged and looked away from us. She hadn't hesitated to share, but I knew that look on her face. She had opened up, actually spoken to me, and she regretted it. Nancy needed a distraction and not someone to keep asking how she felt and show her sympathy. She didn't want it. She didn't want to cry in front of us.

Quickly I looked over Eddel and the mismatched clothes she wore that were partly my father's and partly my mother's that had been gathered from somewhere in my house and then quickly counted how much money my mother had given me. Surprised to find a few hundred dollars in my hand, I shoved it back in my pocket as if someone would take it from me and I said, "Let's go shopping for Eddel!"

"What?" Eddel looked at me.

Lilias nodded and agreed. "Yi'll need somethin' better 'an peasant claes!"

Claes... what the hell were claes? There was a pause among

132

all of us where I watched a similar thought cross our minds, all except Lilias. I hoped she meant clothes. I needed a Scottish to American dictionary. Or she needed to enunciate. Something told me it would only make it funnier if she tried to hit all of her consonants.

That was the perfect distraction for Nancy and she appeared relieved as we entered through the automatic doors and rushed up the stairs. I thought the doors opening on their own would frighten Eddel but she was used to magic so it actually didn't faze her. The inside of the mall gave her pause. All of the people, all of the echoing noise, all of the stark white walls and colorful clothes and storefronts.

I took Eddel's hand in mine and skipped forward in front of her. "Come on!"

I was excited. I had been in the mall hundreds of times, but this was the first time that I could show this to someone. I could explain things. I could help. This was brand new for Eddel and I told her I wouldn't leave her behind.

Eddel reached a hand out to Nancy, who took Lilias's hand, and finally Chandra brought up the end of the chain. We walked five abreast when we could, not a single one of us straggling behind. We crowded among one another staring at cute clothes on mannequins and *ooh*ing and *ahh*ing over things in the candy shops. A curious thing to be noted, even Eddel avoided the little kiosk stands in the middle of the walkways. She didn't have to be told not to make eye contact with the salespeople. Avoiding them was a universal decision as we all briskly walked past them. I had to laugh. None of us were so different from one another.

Shopping for Eddel was like a game show. We ran through the racks in department stores while Eddel stood dumbfounded. We piled clothes in her open arms and over her shoulders and steered her to the fitting rooms. The others stood about and waited for her to show her new looks and I sat on the floor like a heathen. One outfit after another we gave our thumbs up and thumbs down like emperors at the Colosseum, but instead of gladiators, it was fashion night. Eddel was a fashion knight.

When we had a few things, I paid and escorted Eddel to the bathroom to change. I stayed by the sinks and mirrors and waited. I crossed my arms and felt a little bruise and it was only then that I noticed my reflection. This tanned and bruised person looking back at me was actually me. I looked like a menace. The other girls weren't mottled in purples and blues. If people had been staring at me, I had been too distracted to notice.

My skin was darker from all of my time outside. Magical village or not, I had still soaked in plenty of sun. The bruises on my arms were from sword fighting practice with Valeria. She had a habit of using the flat of her blade in the most humiliating ways when I lost my focus. The bruise I had felt was along my right forearm from where my horse had dragged me under trees and I had put my hands up to protect my face. Saoirse had said I wasn't paying attention. I probably wasn't. And then there was the long blackening bruise on my left wrist from forgetting to use the guard while playing with a bow. I hadn't picked one up since. Admittedly I wasn't the best with a sword, or a horse, and pretending to be Hawkeye was not going to happen. My luck was already being expended elsewhere, I didn't need to push it.

Running my hands over my arms, I felt muscles where there once had been none. I flexed my right hand and could see the different muscle groups along my forearm. I turned left, turned right, gazing at my reflection. I was surprised my mother hadn't commented on how different I looked instead of how different I sounded. Had she expected me to look different and still be a raging pain in the backside? More than likely.

My eyes were still that odd gray color that they had turned on my birthday and I wondered for a moment if Galahad's eyes had been gray? No, the longer I thought about it, I knew it couldn't be right. Sir Perceval had blue eyes. Eddel's were brown. Sir Gawain had brown eyes. Our Gawain's were green. Whatever this change was in my eyes had little to nothing to do with our ancestors. It made me wonder, why me? Why was I different?

Did this have anything to do with the way that Galahad had died? I chuckled to myself. Yes, I was God's chosen grail knight, and he gave me gray eyes to signify I was weird. I was the chosen one. What a sack…

The sound of the toilet flushing caught my attention. Then I heard another flush and after a moment, another.

"Eddel?" I asked.

"These toilets are amazing!" she laughed from one of the stalls.

There were still wonders in this world.

When I finally managed to pull her away from the magic of modern toilets, we rejoined everyone by the couches outside the restrooms and almost immediately I heard my name. "Socorro?"

The voice didn't come from anyone I had brought with me and I turned stiffly to look in the direction of the caller.

I knew her. She hadn't changed. Emily.

"Oh damn, Em?" I hadn't seen her since I left school, sick on my birthday.

She was still as pale as ever, in that stage most of us passed through in high school where we dyed our hair black. I didn't. My hair was already long and unmanageable and I didn't want to do the upkeep.

She wore her black hoodie, the exact match of the one I had left on my bed at Eddel's. I could have brought it with me but the weather was so unpredictable in Texas this time of the year that I would just be putting it on and taking it off all day.

With Emily was a couple other friends of ours from school: Jake and Gabriella. And then there was Kyle, who was not my friend and wouldn't be hanging out with them if I were still around. There was nothing special about the way they dressed. Darker clothes, blues and blacks, with a little too much eyeliner in all the bad ways around Gabriella's brown eyes. She tried to do the cat eye thing. She failed. Kyle was wearing eyeliner for all the wrong reasons. It looked good on movie pirates, not so much on edgy wannabes with wealthy parents.

"Shit Socorro, you look ripped," Jake said as he came forward and gave me a weird half-surfer high-five handshake. Jake was always cool. He didn't care if people thought he was the odd duck. He redesigned himself every few weeks and played with thrift store outfits made of his most questionable finds. During February, he dressed as a cowboy for the San Antonio Stock Show and Rodeo. He upped the good ol' boy accent for the whole month. He never cared what people thought of him. I had always wanted to be more like him.

"Where've you been?" Emily balked, looking me over. She took a step closer to me, to us, but didn't try to make any kind of contact the way that Jake had.

"Uh..." I drew my shoulders to my ears and ran my hands up my arms as I looked at the others for help. They stared at me. We obviously couldn't tell her the truth, not that they would believe me if I did. "Knight school?"

Someone nudged me from behind.

"Oh..." Emily's hardened gaze of betrayal began to soften. "You're just going to night school to get your GED now since you were failing classes so bad?"

The heirs snickered and I cast them a glare over my shoulder. Emily didn't have to put it like that in front of them, but I deserved it.

"Yeah," I sort of lied. "Night school. I mean really, did any of us expect me to actually walk the stage?"

"I thought you'd figure it out somehow," Jake said. "You always do."

Ah, optimistic Jake. He was great. He reminded me of a less mysterious version of Gawain. Both were the friendly sort. Unlike Gawain, Jake's smiles were always genuine. He wore his entire world on his sleeves and he didn't care who saw it.

"You never responded to my texts," Emily said.

Texts... I forgot those were a thing. I carried my phone with me for music and didn't remember until that moment that it was still a communication device.

"Oh..." I pulled my phone from my back pocket and realized I had left it off after charging it at my mother's house. Turning it on, I put it back in my pocket and said, "It's been off for a while."

"You're really bad about keeping in touch with friends," Eddel muttered at my side. "Even when you're living with them."

That was a deep wound. She had noticed my distance

while I was training. Of course she had. I hadn't focused on any of my friendships, and had the proof on my arms that I wasn't focused during my lessons. What had I even been doing? I had been studying my ass off and what did I have to show for it? Nothing I did was good enough.

"What? Why'd you turn it off?" Emily complained. She hadn't heard Eddel.

"Money?" I said. "Can't always afford it. It's expensive." My phone had been turned off quite a few times over the years. Cell phones were a luxury I didn't always have.

Kyle snorted, "Tell your deadbeat parents to get a job."

The couches rustled and my fellow heirs rose to their feet. I felt them all at my back. My heart was in my throat. I wasn't sure if they were there to support me in my desire to stomp my foot through Kyle's gut, or to hold me back. Either way, I felt relief that they were even there at all. I was terrible with friendship. I was thankful that they valued mine.

Pride. There were seven deadly sins that Merlin had taught me. This day, pride attempted to surface. I wanted to save face. I wanted to take his words and make him regret them. Perhaps it was his pride that fought mine.

The repeated dinging of my phone pulled my attention away from my thoughts. Kyle wasn't worth my time and this wasn't a fight that needed to be fought.

I smiled instead and told him, "Hey Kyle? You say that again and I'll show you how I got these bruises on my arms."

Eddel's hand went to my shoulder and her fingertips pressed into my skin. When I lived in this world, that wasn't a threat I would act on. The version of me that lived with Eddel might have meant it. Eddel believed I meant it.

"Oh please," Kyle sighed. "My father would sue your pants off if you laid one finger on me."

Petty. I wanted to rise to it. My jaw hurt from clenching my teeth and there was a little niggling thought in the back of my head that was confident that, not only could I punch his face into his skull, I also had the means to hide the evidence. I didn't think that was one of my own thoughts, maybe that was Galahad.

I looked at Emily with my brows furrowed and tilted my head toward Kyle. I didn't have to say anything. Sometimes we could talk all day without words. We had known one another since we were itty bitty preschoolers.

Gabriella said, "We're dating now."

An involuntary, "Ew," passed my lips. I didn't regret it.

Gabriella held his hand and laid her head on his shoulder. My nose wrinkled and I whistled lowly.

Lilias chuckled somewhere behind me. Even her laugh had an accent.

Shaking my head, I took a deep breath and told Emily, "I'll try and return texts before I lose my phone again."

"Is it that bad?" Emily asked. "At home?"

"Nah, man. My mom's doing pretty good now," I said and left it at that. Emily and Jake knew how bad things could get with my father. I wished I was able to tell them more, assure them that I was fine and I would see them again as soon as I could.

"We need to hang again," Jake said and gave me another quick half-handshake half-high five. He held no grudges about my lack of communication.

"Yeah yeah," I confirmed. I wasn't sure when it could happen, but I wanted to see them again. "For sure. Hopefully sooner rather than later."

"Cool," he said with a smile. "You got my number. Don't be a stranger now."

"I'll see you guys around," I told them and started walking. It was an abrupt cut to our conversation If I stayed it would only get weirder, more uncomfortable, and much more difficult to explain. They wouldn't understand this new world I had been sucked into, and I doubted the heirs would be very accepting of outsiders knowing people like us even existed.

As we passed Kyle, he stepped out and checked me with his shoulder. I staggered, and when my gaze landed on him again, he was flinching from Chandra's raised fist. Lilias was laughing at him and even Nancy was sticking her tongue out and making a face. Eddel was at my side with a soft, "You alright?"

"Yeah," I said and shrugged it off. "Yeah, no big. He's a short little fucker."

The girls were giggling as we walked away.

I had never had people that would actually fight for me before. I wanted to deserve this kind of friendship.

As we hit up the fudge shop, the ice cream shop, and the cookie kiosk, I wondered how it was that I had become so open to strangers and so closed to friends. Though, these four with me were no longer strangers. They were as close as family, even if whatever presence that was Galahad had some kind of influence over that. We shared a secret home, a secret way of life that no one else outside of it could ever hope to understand. I had lived there for over a month and sometimes I felt that I was no closer to understanding what we were or who we used to be. All I knew was that when I was with them, it felt like family.

"I'm proud of you," Eddel told me when we stood waiting for Lilias, Nancy, and Chandra as they poked around a shop full of delightful smelling bath products.

140

"What?" I asked.

"You know, you say that so often that even I've started responding with 'what'."

I smirked. "Oops."

"I meant," she began again, "I thought you were going to hit him."

"He wasn't worth it," I said as I crossed my arms. I remembered my bearing, the way Valeria had taught me and dropped my hands to my sides. Not sure what to do with them, I set my fingers in the back pockets of my jeans.

Drawing my shoulders forward, I told her, "Kyle's always been a weasel. He threatened to sue me in second grade when I didn't give him back a pencil I borrowed. He's a dick."

"You're coming along very quickly," she said.

"In what?" I asked.

"Your training. One day you'll swear the oath like the rest of us, or at this rate, before most of us. I'm impressed." She gave a soft chuckle and added, "I think Henry would have hit him."

"I'd love to have seen Kyle say any of that to Henry," I chuckled. Though I didn't imagine our dear heir of King Arthur saying much of anything to a squealing pig like Kyle. Henry was still an intimidating figure when he wanted to be.

"Speaking of Henry…"

I raised a brow. "Yea?"

"The two of you have seemed a bit… closer since you woke up from your death nap," she said.

Closer? I didn't understand her definition of close. I hadn't spoken to much of anyone while throwing myself into every lesson in a desperate attempt to catch up to the other heirs. I suppose I might have acknowledged his existence with a nod here and there in passing.

"Death nap?" I asked. "Is that what you're calling it?"

She shook her head. "You called it that. So everyone else started to as well."

"Huh…" I exhaled. I didn't remember ever calling it a death nap, but if Eddel said I did, then I probably did. Her memory was always better than mine.

"You're deflecting," she said.

"About Henry?" I scoffed. "No. Look. Merlin has his rules. You told me them yourself. I didn't realize we were acting close. I guess if it's a problem I'll—"

"No," she said quickly, shaking her head. "I was only being cautious."

I cast a smirk to Eddel and asked, "Cautious? Or… just a little jealous?"

I was teasing of course, but Eddel didn't seem to understand the joke. She stared at me blankly and replied, "Why would I be jealous?"

"Ouch." I feigned offense and rubbed at my heart a moment before I shook my head and sighed, "I'm not planning on getting kicked out so soon by rule breaking."

"Says the woman that was moments ago talking about searching out the borders."

"Is that against the rules?"

Eddel smirked. She turned away from me then to check on the others and as I looked out across the crowded mall, I frowned. People were waving at me.

CHAPTER NINE

Party Crashers

"For fuck's sake!" I cried out and Eddel's attention shot to me. I gestured out ahead of us where two men approached. Henry and Gawain had followed us to the real world.

"This is a girls only outing," Eddel told Henry when they were close enough that she didn't have to shout.

"We're not following you home," Gawain assured us. "Just getting out and stretching our legs a bit." He made a show of lifting his knees as he marched in place.

"And what's wrong with stretching your legs back at the village?" Eddel shot back.

"This seemed like more fun?" Gawain said with a sheepish smile.

"Go home," Eddel ordered and pointed them back the way they came.

"Come on, Eddel," Henry pleaded. "Merlin would only let us out if we joined up with you."

"Then go back," she told them with a dismissive wave of her hand.

Their faces were entirely crestfallen. Out here, even as inexperienced as she was, Eddel was still somehow in charge of everyone. Even Henry.

"Please?" they pleaded, drawing out the word, grinning like fools.

Eddel looked at me.

I shrugged. "Who are we to deny our brothers-in-arms succor?"

Her brows furrowed deeply. "I'm going to talk to Merlin about your lessons."

"What about them?"

"He's doing too good a job," she muttered.

For a moment, it felt as if we had swapped places, I was the patient and giving one and she was... whatever I was.

"Think of it this way," I said, "I don't think my mom can fit all of us in the car sooo they're stuck here when we leave. They'll have to portal home."

Eddel hadn't thought of that and she grinned broadly. "Good."

"Aw that's mean," Gawain pouted.

"Safety first," I told him.

What I didn't expect was for my mother to pull up in the car later that afternoon and say, "I'm sure we can fit everyone."

We crammed into the car. We were a complete safety hazard. This should never have been done. That being said, I was glad again to be in the front seat. I was amazed to see Eddel sitting squeezed behind me with Henry behind my mother and Nancy sitting on Lilias and Chandra's laps, squeezed in the middle like a tiny pyramid. Across everyone's knees in the most agonizing half curled position, was Gawain.

"I'm going to need a chiropractor," he groaned.

Nancy had wanted to go to the movies. We went to the movies. I knew the heirs occasionally left the village, but the

144

way they acted when I bought the tickets was like they never got the chance to go anywhere at all. I wondered if they did get to leave and were still restricted to wherever their parents were. My mom was more than happy to take me places with my friends and leave me there. That was another way I was different from the others. Their parents liked to hover the way Merlin did. The heirs were important to them, important for whatever Merlin needed us for.

What exactly did he need us for?

Why were the heirs created? And why now?

I had already seen this particular movie, so I led them to our seats and went back for refreshments. No one offered to come with me, and I was a bit glad for that. I needed a breather. I had wanted to bring people with me so I wouldn't feel alone in this world, but I still needed some time to myself. Even if it was mere seconds.

Everyone wanted a drink. I was going to give the heirs so much sugar that I wondered if they would get sick. They deserved a chance to be unsupervised kids. This was a few hours of not being an heir to this or that. I delivered their drinks first and smiled as I returned to the concessions stand with a bounce in my step for their popcorn and candy.

There was a young man in front of me in line waiting on his own popcorn to pop. The theater was surprisingly busy for a Wednesday afternoon and the staff hadn't had the chance to throw more in to cook. They were running back and forth like busy little bees. The man sighed as the lady behind the counter asked him to step to the side and for me to come forward.

I counted on my fingers and decided we could share large popcorn tubs and asked for four. "There will be a little bit of a wait," she said sadly.

"Yeah, that's fine," I replied. I understood. I wasn't about to gripe at the worker bees for a problem that was out of their control. In the meantime I bought the candy and took up counter space at a respectful distance from the man that had been ahead of me. I glanced down to the line at my left and found people waiting there as well. The great popcorn depression of 2018 was in full swing.

"Have we met?" I heard. He was trying to talk to me.

I hadn't seen his face but I replied, "Nope," just the same.

"Are you sure?" he asked.

"I'm sure of it," I said shortly. If he kept talking to me, I was going to lose my patience.

"How sure?" he asked.

I snapped my attention to him with a sharp reply on the tip of my tongue and I froze. His long dark hair was tied back at the nape of his neck. He wore a v-neck black shirt and jeans and appeared as ordinary as anyone else standing in a line. I had seen him and I had ignored him. I thought he was a nobody like me.

"Hi Galahad," he said with a coy smile playing across his lips.

My breath returned from wherever it had been hiding and I swallowed hard as his light blue eyes, speckled with gold dust, stared deep into my soul. His smile would have been charming if I didn't feel like it belonged to a snake. There were fangs there, even if I couldn't see them. His face was different but I knew him just the same.

"Mordred," I said and was immediately calmed by the steadiness of my own voice. This was not the same outsides of the man I had encountered in Galahad's memories. The insides might not have been exactly the same either, but somewhere deep inside was that blue-eyed traitor that filled a small part of me with a range of emotions I couldn't hope to decipher.

I watched him pop a mini peanut butter cup into his mouth and chew slowly. My hand balled into a fist. I wanted to punch him in the mouth but I rolled my shoulders back instead and tried to ease the tension that threatened to push me over a threshold that I needed to maintain in public.

"I love these things, don't you?" he asked, an accent to his words I hadn't heard before. I hadn't heard many accents before and I certainly couldn't place his. "Where are my manners..." he muttered and offered me his hand. "Murphy."

I didn't return the pleasantries. I stared at him the way Galahad had once done to Mordred in the woods in the shadow of Camelot.

"Oh don't look at me that way," he said. "I didn't betray *you*."

Meaning, he had still betrayed someone.

"What are you doing here?" I asked. My teeth hurt from clenching my jaw.

"Investigating," he said simply. "Reconnaissance." He ate another piece of chocolate and then added. "Now that you're all together, it's only a matter of time before we find out where you're hiding."

"Hiding?" I asked.

"Merlin can't conceal your little village forever," he told me as casually as he ate his candy. "The stronger you heirs of the Round Table grow, the less he can protect you. I imagine he didn't want you out here alone so he sent you with your little friends." He shook his head and made a soft *tsk*ing noise with his tongue on his teeth. "And here you are. On your own."

I risked taking my eyes off him. The lobby was completely still. Nothing moved, everyone was frozen in time. I didn't know if this version of Mordred had some command of magic, but if he didn't, he was in league with someone who did.

I was glad my hands were already in my pockets. He couldn't see them tremble this way.

Taking a deep breath to steady my nerves, I said, "You're making my popcorn take longer."

His charming smile faltered and was replaced by confusion.

Mordred, or rather, Murphy, was in the same age range as the others. Probably older than me, but not Eddel. "What...?" he said softly.

I waved a finger around and gestured at the room. "My popcorn is taking longer. If you can freeze time, can you speed it up so we can be done with this conversation?"

"I—" his voice failed him. The world around us clicked back into motion.

"Cool," I said. "Thanks," and turned back to the lady to watch her hand him his tub. I stuffed a few packs of candy into my pockets and when she brought the four to me, I pinched them with my fingers and tried not to spill more than was necessary.

As I slowly sifted them under the butter machine, he came to me again.

"You're not—?"

"Afraid of you?" I asked, still monitoring the butter to popcorn ratio. When I was satisfied with one, I set it aside and worked on another. "No. Why?"

"We're enemies?" he said. "You side with Merlin, and I with Morgan le Fay."

"Yeah, okay," I said. I had gathered that much. This wasn't new information to me, though I wasn't exactly sure who Morgan le Fay was. I knew of Mordred from Galahad's history. I had asked Merlin about him and only been given about as much information as I had gathered from my conversation with Henry. As for the sorceress Morgan le Fay? Aside from knowing we were at odds and she was a sorceress, that was the extent of that story. Merlin had not been very forthcoming with anything beyond a very basic who. He left out the what, where, when, and why.

"You should be royally freaked out!" he huffed.

Pausing, I set my popcorn down and put my hand on my hip. "Why? You're the heir of Mordred, yeah?" He nodded slowly. "I'm the heir of Galahad. I'm just about the only knight that survived the last round of bullshit and had to pray for my own death. What makes you think you're going to win round two, hundreds of years later?"

He was silent, his lips parted.

"That's what I thought." I left it at that and returned to my popcorn.

He didn't say anything else, and when I finished and grabbed the buckets, I discovered he had left.

The movie had already started by the time I returned to the others. They hadn't noticed. They were too excited to have popcorn and candy to realize it had taken so long.

"I never get to have popcorn," Gawain said happily and proceeded to cram a handful into his primary face-hole.

Glancing down the line from where I sat, watching the light of the screen shine on their happy faces, I decided it would be best to withhold the information I had gained. I'd let them have their moment.

I tried to watch the movie, but my thoughts were racing.

The heirs of the Knights of the Round Table had to be together again because we were going to war. We were finishing a battle from long ago where Mordred had fatally wounded King Arthur. Morgan le Fay was back. Mordred was back. Would the once and future king return to lead us into battle? Or would this be fought with children whom had been raised from birth for this very reason?

I had some unkind words for Merlin.

CHAPTER TEN

Purpose

I let them enjoy their movie, but it wasn't long after that they noticed I wasn't talking much. Not that I was a regular social butterfly. I tried to keep the mood going, smiling as they discussed the film, nodding as if I were listening. There was too much on my mind. They had to know, and I hated the thought that the knowledge would bring this adventure of ours to a close. We hadn't been out of the village more than a day. If I told them, we would undoubtedly be going back.

My mother picked us up from the movie theater and we crammed into the car. The thunderstorm had ceased while we were in the theater and the night evening sky was cloudy. I stared out the window the entire trip back to the house as a headache banged on the sides of my brain.

I dragged my feet as I left the car. How did I tell them? If I already came to a negative conclusion with the limited knowledge I had, how were they going to feel?

The Texas evening had begun to cool but the rain had kicked up the humidity. We filed out of the car and I felt my skin start to feel a little oily. I paused, watching them all file up to the house and then smelled the sweet scent of the white flowers on the magnolia tree in the front yard. It was planted for my grandmother, my mom's mom. I closed my eyes, bringing in the perfume that would carry through summer.

There was magic here too, though it was faint. The light of the waxing gibbous moon. The glow of early lightning bugs, the grow of grass. The smell of the ground, the asphalt of the road. Dirt. I could smell the wet dirt in the yard where the rain flooded the grass and settled deep into the soil. It had been a good, soaking rain.

"Sox?"

Gawain backtracked towards me, his boots squishing in the mud. We had to walk through the lawn to get to the house. My mother had to park on the street because my father had two old trucks sitting in the driveway. They didn't run, and I had heard them argue so many times about what he was going to do with them.

"Everything okay?" Gawain asked.

Past him, everyone hesitated to cross the threshold into my house. They stood on the front porch watching me. My silence had been noticed. I wasn't good at hiding that there was something wrong. Wasn't I good at that in the past? Or was it as simple as no one had cared to pay attention before? I wasn't a window to these people.

I waved for them to head inside. I meant to follow them in, but Gawain waited for me to step even with him and his hand reached out to me. His fingertips grazed my shoulder.

"Hey—" he began.

I risked a glance to him and gently shook my head. I didn't want to repeat myself. Getting this all out once was trouble enough. I still didn't know what to say.

Inside, no one sat. My mother saw our odd behavior and

hovered by the kitchen table. She gave us space, though not enough to be completely cut out of the conversation. I realized I wanted her input. I could have used anyone and everyone's input. I didn't know what was going on. All I knew was something felt wrong, as if the world was too quiet outside. Or I was too quiet inside.

"I've got some news," I said and they shifted where they stood. They were attentive, though they glanced to one another with trepidation.

I told them about Murphy. I told them everything he said, and when I was finished, Eddel replied, "I had a feeling… this is what was going on."

"What is going on?" I asked.

Henry sighed, "All this time, I knew the war wasn't over. We've been at a ceasefire until the armies were rebuilt."

Nancy sat down on the couch in silence. She hung her head. She couldn't catch a break. She had no outside family anymore, and her new family expected her to fight, to risk her life in the same way that they would risk theirs. Any of us could die. All of us could die.

Lilias took a deep breath. "Alright…" she said and for a second I thought she would say more. She didn't.

Even Chandra's quiet reservation had taken on a new feeling. She stared across the room at the wall as if gazing through it. Had she disappeared into some memory? Lost to thought in ways I couldn't imagine?

Gawain was silent. His face was taut and entirely unreadable. But I thought I knew why. They said he lost his mind a bit when he read of what his ancestor might have done. The war returned and he was doomed to repeat it. We all were. And not a single one of us had an heir of our own.

This was the end of the line. We were Merlin's cannon

153

fodder.

My mother didn't say anything. I think she knew that no matter what she said, it wouldn't make a difference. I didn't care whether or not she knew. She hadn't raised me like the others had been raised. We had tough times as I grew up, especially with my father's absence. There had been some good times sprinkled in there, times of laughter that I thought about with a heavy heart as I stood among my fellow heirs. I had been raised with freedom from ever knowing what I was meant for and perhaps that was a blessing. Ignorance is bliss, as it were.

The original plan had been to camp at my house for a few more days. My information had killed our trip. Murphy was a buzzkill.

My mother sent us each through the portal with a strong hug. She held me especially tight and said, "We'll get through this."

I didn't know exactly what 'this' was but I had an idea. She sent me with a bowl of cookies.

"That's my good bowl," she told me. "You have to bring it back, Socorro." She looked to the others and said, "And all of you have to help her bring it back, okay?"

Solemn nods and faint smiles were their only responses.

Henry summoned the portal at the doorway to my laundry room and we crossed back into our valley village where the sun was still up for a few hours more. Henry was right, there was no use in trying to figure out how a day worked in the sanctuary compared to the outside world.

Silence followed us as we made our way from the arches. We must have looked like we had something to say and people fell in line around us as we walked. Their murmurs filled the air with a soft hum. We gained a tail of heirs and

154

villagers, and I held the bowl of cookies to my chest.

Some kind of call must have gone out, though I didn't hear a thing. Maybe it was the fact that the village was small and we were a moving mass that forced everyone to meet us at the pavilion where we shared our meals.

I could hear the whispers of the people around us as Eddel brought us to a stop.

"What's going on?"

"This doesn't feel right."

"Look at their faces…"

I looked at the friends I had come back with. They weren't smiling. I had never seen them so grim. They were much taller than I felt. They were like titans, and I a mere mortal.

"Merlin!" Eddel called out and the sorcerer came forward.

"Eddel?" he asked. He seemed surprised at her tone.

Her demeanor had changed and the old man showed his concern. I felt it. Eddel had never spoken to him in such a way, not in front of me. I was the only one that had openly challenged him, many had told me that. The whispers of the elders had echoed that sentiment time and time again.

"Morgan le Fay is on the move," she said and a hush fell over the crowd around us.

Henry stepped forward then. "If she has built an army, our presence here will not go unnoticed."

The heirs began speaking and a commotion rose around us until I couldn't hear myself think. Merlin raised a hand and it quieted to near silence.

"Is this what we were raised for?" Eddel questioned. "The second round of a war that started ages before we were born?"

Merlin's face was impassive. He gave us nothing.

Eddel continued, "What life have we had, Merlin?"

I felt myself tremble at her accusation.

"You wish to leave?" Merlin finally asked.

Eddel looked over us. Her attention lingered on me and jumped away to the next face. "I can't speak for everyone," she told him. "But I cannot sit back and wait to see what Morgan le Fay does to the world outside this one. I know what I am. I am Eddel Lebna, the heir of Sir Perceval. What I want now, Merlin, is to know who I am. I cannot live under the shadow of the Knights of the Round Table. I must know my own heart. And so must we all if we wish to stand a chance at winning. We must know what sways us, where we stand strong and where we fold, only then can the heirs of Camelot stand in victory."

I wanted to clap. If the bowl hadn't been in my hands, I would have clapped. And then I would have been the awkward one, because it was still silent all around me.

"What is it you wish for?" Merlin asked steadily.

"Less restrictions," Eddel told him. "We are the last heirs. Not a one of us has progeny. I have observed feelings emerging between my fellow heirs. Their love for their comrades will only grow. It will only make us stronger when we have something personal to fight for, and not just someone else's war."

Merlin scowled. He did not like it. "Anything else?" he said tensely.

"Toilets," Gawain declared.

I snickered but many of the heirs cheered.

"Modern music!" Lilias cried out and many agreed.

"Let us be ourselves!" Gabriel pleaded.

"I have never stopped that," Merlin said with a shake of his head.

"Perhaps not consciously," Eddel told him. Once more she

looked over those of us at her side and she made a decision. "We are constantly frightened of disappointing you, and our village. We were raised being told that we are supposed to be like long dead ancestors. I am tired of walking on eggshells for your approval."

"Oh shit…" I whispered before I could stop myself.

"As am I," Henry agreed.

When the heir of King Arthur spoke, it broke the spell of caution over us and the heirs found their voices.

"Let us make mistakes!"

"Let us be kids!"

Gawain said, "Let us have control over our own lives. I don't want to be Sir Gawain. I want to be me!"

Silence. There was solidarity in that quiet. I held my breath. I thought I would be too loud if I used my lungs at all.

"Regardless of the paths we take," Eddel said slowly, "we are all sinners. Christ died for our sins, and God will judge us when we pass on."

Gawain chimed in with, "Which might unfortunately be sooner rather than later…" His humor had turned a little dark, but the tension had already settled around us and it only matched the mood.

I was the only one that hadn't said anything. I remembered to breathe and I took a deep breath to say, "If these terms are satisfied. I'll stay. I'll continue training for… whatever dumbass shit I was born into." Perhaps there was a destiny, and if this was mine, well then I supposed there was no running from it.

If I died before ever seeing my mother again, I hoped she knew I loved her. I hoped she didn't grieve forever. I hoped one day after I was gone, she would learn to smile again and some day even start anew far away from anyone that had ever heard of this place and the heirs of the Round Table.

"I'm in," Gawain agreed. "I mean, what else do I know? And who else would I spend my time with if all of the people that make fun of me… uh, I mean friends, are here?"

I elbowed Gawain and muttered, "Those are two different things? I always thought they were the same."

Humor. This place needed that breath of humor. Nervous chuckles surfaced among the heirs and I felt the crushing weight of our decision begin to ease.

Henry said, "I will stay." He looked among the others and asked, "Will you?"

Mob mentality. Even if someone wanted to leave, everyone declared in that moment that they would remain in the fight. If anyone wanted to go, they wouldn't be able to speak up without feeling othered. I was glad I had already decided to make my bed and lay in it.

With all of our words spoken, our attention turned to Merlin.

"You have made your demands," Merlin told us. "I will allow them."

"Don't forget our toilets!" someone shouted. I thought it might have been Quinn.

"Yeah!" Gawain roared in solidarity.

That was the easiest of the demands.

"Well in that case…" Gabriel said slowly, his voice timid though it rang out as clear as if he too were adamant about toilets. I could hear the words tremble as they passed his lips. We turned to look at him and his short brown hair hung limp around his face. He was a shorter young man, though most of the heirs looked short compared to Henry, Gawain, and Eddel. Why had I befriended the tallest of us all?

"What is it, Gabriel?" Henry asked as he stepped into the

center of the circle with him.

"Um…" Gabriel took a deep breath and glanced around at everyone. "I'm… uh…" He cleared his throat. "I thought… since we're all friends… I thought everyone should know… I'm gay."

I barely heard him, though I glanced to his father Lucas who stood outside of the circle of heirs with a proud smile on his face. He had known, and he was glad that his son no longer felt the need to hide it anymore

There were few gasps among the older villagers, and then the cheers of the heirs overwhelmed it. I didn't know Gabriel very well. Those who did swarmed him with open arms. I stepped away from the mass of support. I didn't want to be crushed to death by their gleeful acceptance.

I couldn't imagine how difficult it was for him to come out. Knights and kingdoms were based in religion. That was how many of them had been raised. We had been given permission to be ourselves and Gabriel took that and didn't look back. I was happy for him.

"You knew?" I asked Eddel. She was the only one that was still close to me.

"No," she said and gently shook her head with a soft smile. "But I'm glad I'm not alone."

"Alone?" I asked.

"I am too," she told me.

I paused. She was too. I smiled.

Touching her finger to her lips to quiet me, she said, "I don't want to take away from his moment."

That was her information to tell or not to tell. Instead, I put the covered bowl under my arm and gave her a hug. "Thank you for getting us toilets."

"Oh that's what you hug me for?" she laughed. "I thought

it was for lifting the relationship ban."

"For me?" I asked and stepped back. "For what?"

She nodded out toward the crowd and I looked to where she gestured.

"Yeah," I said slowly and drew that word out with uncertainty. "A. I don't know who you're nodding toward. Everyone is over in that direction. And two. If I have to put a term to it, I'm like… hard demi on my best days."

Eddel raised a brow. "Demi? You'll have to explain that to me."

For a moment, with her background of being raised by Merlin, I wondered if she thought I meant I was only attracted to demigods. Which, I mean, who wouldn't be?

This was certainly an odd day. At least it felt like a victory.

CHAPTER ELEVEN

Omens

With threat of Morgan le Fay on the surface, attitudes around the village did not change much. Except for the fact that we were encouraged to go about armed and prepared for combat should we be found and forced to engage. We were all together, and we were growing in strength. Murphy had said we wouldn't be protected much longer, which lent the belief that an adversary could enter our hidden world at any time. We had to be ready.

The heirs had swords that were their permanent partners, ones given during ceremony. As the newest unwilling recruit, I had a blank longsword without ornament. I hadn't been there long enough to earn my blade, it came after a year in residence in the village and after a skills test that, according to Valeria, I was nowhere near ready for. That was a bit of a punch to my pride when I thought I was doing quite well. I figured I would probably die before I got more than my practice sword and a borrowed pony.

The next morning, I arrived to my riding lesson and found Saoirse was not there waiting for me. The barn was quiet in the early hours so soon after dawn. The sun had barely broken the horizon and the air was still chilled with the tinge of night and a soft fog that clung to the empty space around me.

On occasion, I had a habit of arriving before Saoirse, and in those instances I tacked up the horses for us. Stepping into the wooden barn, I blinked in the darkness and heard, "Hey."

I nearly leapt out of my skin.

"About time you showed up. Mom said you have a habit of getting here ridiculously early." Gawain finally came into view as he led two horses past me and out of the barn.

"Where's your mom…?" I asked as I followed the horses at a safe distance.

"The village old people are having a meeting," he told me. "They try to do that sometimes and Merlin's decision to grant us more freedoms has their heads swiveling about so fast they might explode. So I told her I'd come out riding with you. You would have thought someone gave her a million bucks."

He held out the reins of a large gray gelding to me to me and I took them. I pet the wide draft horse on the little white spot on his forehead and asked, "What do you mean?"

"How many of the heirs are female?" he asked as he set his reins over his bay mare's neck. She had one eye and Saoirse had said he named her Wallflower. The mare was a long-legged hunter, built nothing at all like a warhorse. A long white blaze ran down her face from the middle of her forehead to the tip of her nose. If he wore armor, she wouldn't be able to take the weight. He had a draft horse for that: specifically the big gray gelding that he had saddled up for me to ride. I had never ridden the gray before, but I imagined it couldn't be too difficult. And I appreciated the trust he put in me to ride his horse without ruining it.

162

"Five…?" I said hesitantly and ran over them in my head. There was me, Eddel, Nancy, Lilias, and Chandra. "Yeah. Five."

Mounting up with a jump and a smooth swing of his leg, Gawain found his stirrup irons with his feet and said, "And how many male?"

"Like, seventy? I dunno." I jumped, trying to get on the massive horse as easy as he did. That simply didn't happen.

Glancing around, I found the mounting block and led the gray over. Gawain had taught him to stand well for his rider to climb aboard and it took me a moment to adjust to how wide I had to sit once I was up there.

"After everyone kind of left last night, I overheard the old people talking," Gawain continued, apparently including his mother in that group. "With the ban on mixing bloodlines lifted, they've got it in their heads to start pushing matches and alliances."

"Well that doesn't seem like a good idea," I said as I adjusted my stirrups and gathered my reins.

"They're idiots. The first thing they think is to start using us against one another," he grumbled. His mare started forward and I gave the gray a tap with my heels and he trotted up beside her.

"You were already asleep," he continued, "No one wanted to wake you or some of the others that called it an early night, but we had a meeting. Whatever happens, friendship, love, whatever, we respect one another first. We can't afford infighting, nor can we afford the bickering of our guardians."

"It's a good decision. In a perfect world it would work," I said as I ran my thumbs over the soft supple leather in my hands. He had worked the reins to velvet with many hours in the saddle.

"You don't think it will work?" he asked. The surprise on his face was clear.

"We're human, and we're young," I said. "To err is human. And if you look at our parents, well…" I shrugged.

Gawain was quiet. "I don't want to screw this up," he said softly.

"Screw what up?"

"This. My place in the village. My life. I don't want to be what those stories say I am," he told me.

"What the hell do those stories even say?" I griped. "What the fuck did you read that has you freaked out like this?"

"You wouldn't understand," he sighed.

"Try me," I scoffed.

Wallflower ground to a halt and the sudden stop made my own horse lock up beneath me. Gawain stared at me, his brows low and his eyes sharp on my face. We glared at one another and I realized in that moment that this wasn't how I wanted our friendship to be. I wanted to snap him out of this, but it wasn't my place.

"I'm sorry," I immediately backed down and shook my head. "You're right, I probably wouldn't understand. But… if you ever feel like talking about it…"

His gaze softened as he breathed deep, his chest swelling before he exhaled the tension between us. "Come on," he said and reined his horse around me with the lightest, almost unnoticeable movement.

The bay mare picked up a trot and I gave the gray permission to keep pace. It was like riding a couch that moved to the sound of thunder. I did not ride a horse, I rode a thunder couch.

Gawain was quiet again and the pace of the horses ate up the ground with an extended trot. Up the valley we went with the ruins of the castle coming closer. The sun rose higher and I sighed as my skin took in the heat. It was warmer that day, nowhere near as warm as Texas, and that made it a pleasant morning.

After a moment, Gawain sped up the pace again and the gray's lumbering lope brought a smile to my face. Gawain held back the mare, keeping her from getting too far ahead.

"What's his name?" I asked between the rocking beats of my horse's canter.

Gawain's attention shot to me as if I had smacked him across the back of his head to get it.

I pointed down to the horse beneath me. "Name?"

"Warden," he said.

Warden the gray. I smirked. "Gray Warden, huh?"

A grin finally crossed his lips. "Yeah," he chuckled.

I didn't realize I was worried when he wouldn't smile until he finally did. I was glad he was still talking to me. Gawain's problems were Gawain's problems and I needed to keep my nose out of them if I wanted to keep my friend.

The mare slowed as we came to a ridge and I pulled Warden back. Single file, we wove back and forth over a worn path on the cliff side. I tried not to look down, tried to focus on the back of Gawain's head as he hummed Dear Maria, Count Me In by All Time Low. It was an odd song to hum. Too many notes to stay recognizable through the whole song without slowing it down.

I wanted to ask where we were headed. I lost sight of the castle once we started on the steep switchbacks. I counted my blessings that Warden was a very sure-footed horse.

Laughter. I heard it and looked up from where my fingers curled in Warden's mane. In front of me was no longer the Gawain of my time, but Sir Gawain of the past.

"Come now, Galahad," he said over his shoulder. "This is not a terrible height."

I didn't want to look, though in that moment, I knew Galahad had looked. I knew he entwined his fingers in the mane of his dark bay steed and gripped tight as if it would keep him from falling to his death. Beneath me was no longer Warden but a stocky bay gelding, a draft breed. My horse had changed color. I wasn't in my own time anymore.

Laughter came from behind me and I knew it was Sir Perceval without looking.

"You should not tease him, Gawain. This is not the best way to get home and you know it!" Perceval called ahead.

"Not the best," Sir Gawain said, "But certainly the quickest!"

Why do we need to get there by the quickest route? Galahad was shouting.

I chuckled to myself. It was nice to hear him distressed.

Sir Gawain's dappled bay turned the last switchback and stepped up onto even ground. My horse followed and I looked up. Out ahead beyond the trees rose the citadel. My heart swelled at the sight of it. I caught my breath. Home. Finally I was home.

Pulling up beside us, the great Sir Perceval reined in his snorting horse and I looked to him. Upon his fair face was a great big grin.

Why are you smiling like that?

"Oh, no reason at all," Perceval replied.

Then, Sir Gawain announced, "Last one to Camelot washes Arthur's undergarments for a week!"

They were off. Galahad tried to call after them. He had to go. I felt it. He had to beat them. He couldn't lose! Not like this. He didn't have to beat both of them, only one of them.

I closed my eyes. Warden wasn't my horse, I couldn't do this race, I couldn't charge ahead the way Galahad wanted me to. I knew this was only a memory of his and I refused to charge into it.

The sound of hoof beats caught my ears. I blinked and time splintered with the past overlaying the present as the Gawain of my time raced ahead of me at a breakneck pace.

"Wait!" I called.

I clicked to Warden and gave him his head and a tap on his sides. The Texan in me shouted, "Yah!" and the massive draft beast was off.

The vision had faded when I had forced it away. Once I participated, it flooded back. The castle lay ahead just beyond the forest and I had to beat Perceval to it. Sir Gawain was in the lead and my old bay gelding was trying his best.

I was not going to lose.

"Trouble keeping up?" Gawain called back to me and I wasn't sure which one had spoken. It was both of them moving in unison. Were they merged the way Galahad and I were?

"You had a head start!" I shouted, or did Galahad shout it?

Did it matter? We were breaking through the trees. I had few moments of clarity of my own time, enough to brace myself for Warden to leap a downed tree or guide him around debris of an age long past.

My head was beginning to ache terribly with this awful double vision of present and past. I was fighting it, trying to hold onto my version of the world.

Sir Gawain pulled up his horse, as did Sir Perceval, as they came to a bridge over a stream. The bridge was full of people. They were engulfed in the crowd and unable to cross. Finally I caught up to them, Galahad caught up to them, and he turned his horse away from the bridge. There was no reason for us all to get stuck there.

Gawain's tall hunter Wallflower balked at the bridge, it was broken in our world. He backed her and asked her to leap it and still she didn't budge.

Camelot was so close. I went the way of Galahad and at a dead sprint asked the monstrous horse beneath me to leap the gap of the stream. Warden cleared it with ease. I didn't have time to wonder how I had sat the jump, Saoirse hadn't taught me to jump.

I saw the road into Camelot before me. I wanted to go home more than anything else in the world and as Warden's hoof clopped on the stone road, I was lost. That one hoof beat blew my world away. Camelot was too strong and so was the lure of Galahad's past. We were the same. I was absorbed into him the way I had been on the edge of the forest.

The large bay beneath me, Galahad's steed, ran along the main thoroughfare to the castle. People rushed from our path. The white stone walls of the castle rose before me and I was not about to lose this race. I didn't dare look back. I didn't want to take my eyes off the prize before me.

Crossing beneath the gate, I pulled the bay horse into the courtyard where stable hands came forward to take my gelding. I swung my right leg forward over the neck of my steed and dropped to the side. My Camelot-red cloak swung down behind me and I patted the hindquarters of my sweating horse as the servants led him away to cool him down.

The walls around me were decorated with columns. The second floor mezzanine had white railing and red banners hung from the banisters. I turned to the path that led down to the massive gate and the sound of racing hoof beats hit my ears as Sir Gawain and Sir Perceval came rushing in. Perceval was second. Sir Gawain had lost.

I laughed, "That will teach you to make bets!"

Galahad's words from my mouth.

Servants took their horses after their feet hit the cobblestones. Their boots tapped toward me. Leather soles. I hated leather soles on riding boots. I always slid. That was my thought, not Galahad's.

"Come," Sir Perceval said with a bright grin. "Let us go tell Arthur the good news."

"What good news?" Sir Gawain muttered. There was an edge to his voice that pulled at me, a tone that wasn't his, that didn't belong to this world. I was entangled in this memory that I could not remember that the Gawain of my world ever existed.

"That his undergarments will be particularly well tended these next few days," Perceval laughed and clapped him on the shoulder.

Sir Gawain hung his head in defeat. He had made the bet and he had lost. I shouldn't gloat, and I didn't, but oh how I wanted to.

Laughing at Sir Gawain's misfortune, we made our way into the castle. Carpeted runners ascended the stairs ahead of us, Camelot-red with gold embroidery. Shields and swords decorated the hall in memory of knights lost and honored in silence and the wavy glass panes lit them in soft, effervescent light that made me feel like we walked through a holy place.

The pale gray floors were well maintained even though the traffic through that hall was often heavy. The floors were swept and scrubbed and my face reflected back at me when I looked over the edge of the carpet. The runner were well kept, though they had faded through the middle from extensive use.

As we crossed into the great hall of the throne room, the banners of the living encircled us. Camelot was proud of its people, proud of the knights that served her. I spotted my own heraldry, a white field with a red cross lain upon it. It stood proudly displayed at the left hand of the queen's throne. They held me in high regard, more than I held for myself. Two down from the right hand of the king's throne was the double-headed eagle, wings outstretched on a field of deep purple. The heraldry of Sir Gawain. Sir Perceval's banner was closer to the throne, more purple, but this time covered in many golden crosses.

There were many banners and I knew the name of every knight that graced those walls, but the empty place beside Arthur's seat spoke volumes. That was the name of a knight that was a knight no more.

"But... My lady, it's a dragon," King Arthur protested to his wife, the queen, as they stood before their paired thrones. He was not dressed as a king and he wore no crown in our presence. This was not a public showing and even a fine circlet had been left behind in favor of his unadorned head.

"Yes," she agreed. Her long dark hair was braided and twined with green cord as it lay over her shoulder. Her fair skin was unblemished and her cheeks were rosy. "A dragon is powerful, but it was a sign of your father. Perhaps it is time we take Camelot under another symbol, and not one of only might."

"But My Lady," Sir Gawain interjected as we neared. "Dragons are also wise."

"Gawain agrees with me," the king said and gestured to his knights.

"Because you are his king," Guinevere sighed.

Arthur looked to us with his brows raised and we got the hint.

"No no," the three of us protested as we fervently shook our heads in disagreement.

"We would never solely defer to Arthur's wishes just because he is our king," Perceval said.

The queen didn't believe us for a moment.

"What would you have it then?" Arthur asked. "Three crowns on a field of blue?"

She stared at him. "It's not the worst idea," she said.

"Then when I die, you can burn every symbol of the dragon and tell the historians to only write about the three crowns in the heavenly sky."

Sir Perceval was shaking, gripping himself tightly in the guise of only having his arms crossed. I bit my bottom lip to keep from laughing. Was this our biggest problem now? The heraldry of Camelot?

Sir Gawain cracked first, a snort that broke every one of us. The king had been serious in his declaration, but even he and the queen were chuckling.

The high frescoed ceiling echoed our humor back to us in the empty hall and when we fell quiet with smiles on our faces, the king said, "How fared your patrol?"

"No sign of Lancelot nor Princess Iona," Sir Perceval replied.

"Good," Arthur smiled. He reached back and took the queen's hand in his.

"Do you believe they are on their way to the Black Spire?" Guinevere asked. She shook her head and held Arthur's hand a little tighter. "I wish we could stop hunting them."

"As do I," Arthur replied softly, patting her hand. "Yet...

there was an uproar when I granted you pardon, my dearest. The kingdom has not forgotten, and neither have our enemies. Not to mention, he was considered once a fugitive some years ago when Princess Iona was my intended. To pardon him again for similar infraction...?"

The king sadly shook his head. Lancelot had taken the blame for many of Camelot's tragedies, but never had Arthur considered him an enemy of the kingdom.

"I know," the queen whispered.

"Speaking of our enemies," I said with Galahad's voice. "We were approached in the forest by Mordred."

The queen clutched to Arthur's arm and the king raised his hand to silence me. "We will speak of this later," he said and changed the entire tone of the room. "Now that the three of you have returned, we must meet."

Arthur left his wife with a chaste kiss upon her cheek and together we strode away. We were expected back upon this day at the end of our patrol, and we were not granted a moment to rest. Thankfully our last few days had been mostly uneventful. We quickened after the king and commotion raised from the end of the hall that grew darker with every step we took. Our path was blocked by a pair of broad, ornately carved doors and Perceval and Gawain stepped forward to pull them open with ease.

The room on the other side was significantly brighter. There appeared to be more windows than walls and they let in the midmorning light from nearly every angle. This had once been the king's solarium and was remodeled to house a great round table where every seat was filled except four.

The others rose at the arrival of their king and sat as he ordered. I stood before my own seat and paused. I did not wish to sit with them. My place at the table was different than theirs. Mine had a name. The Siege Perilous stood at Arthur's side, as mundane in appearance as any other chair. It was not. It never would be. Merlin had created this seat for one singular person, the knight whom would reclaim the holy grail for Camelot. A seat that was fatal to all others. I had avoided taking it in the past, had paced in thought during our gatherings. had only sat once before at Arthur's side, but stalling seemed no longer possible as I hesitated beneath the king's gaze.

I, Sir Galahad, son of Lancelot duLac, could no longer run away from my destiny. No matter how much I did not want it.

A charge of electricity ran up my backside, up my spine, the moment my body took its place. My hands ached. How could this be my responsibility? Why was I born into this? I didn't want it. Galahad had never wanted this.

"Preparations are being made," Arthur announced. "Soon, my brave knights, you shall depart on the greatest quest of our time." The king looked to me and said, "It is time, Galahad."

"Of course, my king," I replied.

"Sox!" came a hoarse whisper, a warning that shot chills up my spine.

My name pulled at me and for a second I saw the castle in ruins, the stones broken around me and the walls crumbled by my feet. I closed my eyes and felt the Siege Perilous drag at my soul, burning into me like a brand.

"Socorro. Don't move. Whatever you do, don't move."

Gawain's voice. I heard it and my stomach lurched. I felt frozen, pulled at the back of my mind as my feet were cemented in the dirt. The Siege Perilous held me and I couldn't fight free.

"I have to go, Galahad," I pleaded. "I have to go back."

My mind snapped back into my body and I wheezed. My lungs struggled to work. Had I stopped breathing?

The next breath I took was slow and deep I opened my eyes to see the once polished marble darkened and fractured beneath my boots. Before me lay a stone circle, a massive table that had split in three. A creature stood upon it, a beast, a monster of the likes I had never seen. Its serpent head snaked back and forth, observing me while the tail of its leopard body swished in interest.

The creature's forked tongue flicked out, tasting the air between us. I held still. No quick movements. It hissed softly and the sound washed over me, setting the tiny hairs all over my body on end. I wasn't a fan of snakes, and I wasn't a fan of whatever this thing was. My skin crawled beneath its gaze.

I expected a creature with a snake head and a leopard body to make sounds similar to its components. It did not remind me of either of those things. A low rumbling started in its belly and built to a roar like its insides were filled with hounds baying on a hunt and the foxes they chased screeching and angrily yipping back.

My insides wanted to be my outsides. I wanted to be anywhere but in front of that thing. There was nowhere to run to without it chasing me.

The monstrous chimaera shifted where it stood, and slunk down from the fractured table with low, long steps. The body of the beast wasn't all leopard. The back half lacked spots. The tail reminded me of a lion and the legs belonged to a large deer.

"What the fuck..." I whispered and its serpent head swung back to look at me. A tiny, terrified Socorro reflected in its

174

slitted pupils.

Merlin had said that nothing in this place would harm me. As this creature stared me down, I knew that was no longer true. We had been infiltrated. Murphy had said this would happen.

I watched its legs shift beneath it, saw its body lower and prepare to lunge. My hand went to my unnamed sword and I drew it as the monster sprang from the rubble.

Something slammed against my side and I hit the ground. The blade clattered from my hand and spun away to the castle debris. Metal sang from a sheath as Gawain drew his sword and a monstrous roar answered the call to war. I scrambled for my sword, barely drawing up my legs before a pair of cloven hooves smashed the ground where my knees had been.

Gawain engaged with the beast. He was quick on his feet and used the rubble to keep the distance between himself and the serpent head that lashed at him.

The noon sun was high in the sky and it cast its brightest rays of light down on the heir of Sir Gawain. I was in awe. His blade flashed. Each step he took was graceful like a dancer and each swipe of his sword was sharp and precise. The beast was trying, but it couldn't predict what direction he was going. Gawain was poetry in motion.

Finally I clambered to my feet and took up my sword. That was the wrong move. I was the weaker of the two of us. The monster turned and came after me. I staggered back, falling over myself until my back struck rock.

The beast descended upon me, lunged at me. The sound in its belly grew to a deafening bray.

I was prey.

The serpent head lashed back at its hindquarters with a

pained yowl. Gawain had it by the tail.

"Run!" he shouted.

"Not without you!" I wouldn't leave him here to fight this thing all alone. He needed help.

"You're not good enough!" he shouted.

His words struck me. They were a fist directly into my heart and my hand gripped my sword as ice flooded my veins with frozen spikes. I was trying. Couldn't he see I had been trying to catch up? All of those lessons couldn't have been for nothing. Even though everyone kept encouraging me, I was not a fighter and had never pretended to be one. But there were other ways I could help, weren't there?

"Run, you idiot! I can't hold it forever!"

The beast stepped back and Gawain ran to the side, wrenching on its tail to throw off its balance. The serpent head snapped back at him and the sounds from within screeched and barked so loud it echoed off of the stones around us. I felt it vibrate through my boots and shake the skin on my bones.

The snake head clacked its razor teeth at his hands and Gawain recoiled, abandoning his hold in favor of his fingers. The monster was free. Gawain became its target.

Gawain staggered and took up his sword as he bolted away. The monster followed and any time it seemed to check on me, Gawain threw a rock or made a sound. He was trying to lead the creature away from where I stood with my feet rooted to the ground.

I was no longer held by fear. Anger welled up within me, greater than any emotion I had felt before. Tears brimmed in my eyes and my heart pounded in my ears. Gawain's words had hurt. I wasn't useless.

I had lost count of how many times my father said I wasn't

enough. I was not a boy. I was not him. I was too loud. Too stupid. Too slow. Too lazy. He drilled it into my head until I was too paralyzed to even try anymore. He made me small. He made me insignificant and I was content to let the world pass me by because I hated myself. I would never be what he wanted me to be, so how could I ever be good enough... for anyone?

I reached up and felt the white scars across my shoulder, the ones I gave to myself on those days that seemed bleaker than others. The ones that dug deep enough to draw blood. They only had to be in another place to really make a difference.

Watch for an opening.

An opening...? I could do that.

I clutched my sword in my hand. I was going to help.

The road to hell was paved with good intentions.

The chimaera struck out at Gawain. It reared and a cloven hoof knocked the blade from his hand. He dove for it and the beast went for him. I saw my chance.

I rushed the monster with my sword drawn and buried the blade up to the hilt just behind its elbow. I heard a scream. It could have been the monster, or it could have been me. Or more likely, it was both of us. Blood gushed to the ground beneath the beast. I felt it running down my skin from thousands of punctures along my abdomen. It had seen me after all, had whipped its head around the moment my blade ran it through. It had me in its jaws, squeezing hundreds of tiny dagger-like teeth into my body and I cried out in agony.

I was lucky it had no fangs.

The beast wavered and fell to the ground, its jaws releasing me as it collapsed. My sword was still deep in its carcass and I stood motionless, gripping the hilt tightly. I was unable to let it go.

I had slain the monster. But… at what cost?

Laughter filled the air, a soft feminine sound that rolled over my skin like streams of velvet. My skin reacted in goosebumps.

The monster faded before my eyes, turned to dust and drifted away. There was no sign of its blood on the ground, nor on my sword. There was no sign it had ever been there at all and I was the only one bleeding.

My gaze stayed on the ground where my enemy had once been. I didn't want to look anywhere else. I didn't want to see the damage it had done to me. If I didn't look, then it was nothing but a scratch. I just needed an alcohol swab and bandage and I would be back to myself in no time.

Across the rubble, Gawain's wide eyes stared back at me and I tried not to think about the hot, viscous liquid that ran down my skin and adhered my shirt to my body. There wasn't an I-told-you-so on his lips but he had every right to say it. I had gotten hurt when Gawain had told me to run. He had been right. This battle had been out of my league and I was an idiot.

My hands felt cold and I adjusted my grip. My palms were white with the force I clung to the sword with.

The clattering of hooves up the broken road made me turn. My sword was raised to fight whatever came at us. The sight of Merlin, my father, and another old man on horseback didn't ease the urge to defend myself. These were not friends. I didn't even know the third man. He was olive-skinned and older than my father. There were wrinkles at the corners of his brown eyes that held nothing but grim disapproval.

"Ilar!" my father shouted.

Keep your guard up.

I had every intention to.

My shoulders squared as I held my sword at the ready, eying the man that I called father as he dismounted his horse and stalked towards me.

"Stop!" Gawain ordered. "Don't take another step. Keep your distance! Something's wrong."

My father stepped back.

What was wrong? Wasn't this what they wanted for me? Covered in blood, sword in hand, capable of putting myself in harm's way? Wasn't this the Camelot way?

Merlin stayed upon his horse. He was cautious as he spoke to me. "Socorro...? Are you... can you hear me?"

"The fuck is happening to me?" I yelled in a mixture of anger and despair.

Merlin's brows dipped momentarily in relief and then pinched together in worry. Almost coldly, he said, "We should get that injury looked at."

His words were monotonous, distant.

"Merlin—" began to third man.

"This is not the time," the wizard replied shortly.

"I'll get the horses," Gawain told them, but he didn't go anywhere.

I didn't look at him. I didn't want his horse. I didn't want to go with them. I didn't want to hear all the ways I had done this wrong. There was something going on in my head, something that made me different than the other heirs. I saw the past and walked in Galahad's footsteps. I heard voices, stronger than the mild feelings of guidance they had started as. I was broken.

I needed to get away from them. I needed to be somewhere else. There had to be someone out there that understood me.

Do not run away.

I wasn't running. I was walking. I didn't feel the pain in my body and I attributed that to adrenaline, or to heartache. I didn't belong here. I never did.

I turned my back on them. First came the rapid heavy step of boots.

"Erik!" Merlin shouted.

Steel rang sharply against steel and only then did I stop and look back. Gawain had crossed swords with my father and they were locked hilt to hilt. The sun was still bright and strong and Gawain's strength matched it.

The third man bellowed, "Erik! That is enough!" and Gawain seized that moment to plant his foot squarely into my father's stomach and launch him into the rubble.

Gawain lowered his sword at an angle behind me. He was not stepping down from any additional fights but warning them to keep their distance from both of us.

"Socorro," Gawain whispered over his shoulder. He turned slowly to face me. He held out his empty hand, asking me to stay, asking me to come back with him.

"Stay away from me."

I was incapable of being more than a dirty window. I was not Galahad. I was not capable of surviving the second round of this war. I would die and I was going to get everyone around me killed.

I held my side as the pain began to cut through me like a hot knife. My insides burned and my lungs shook with each breath. I wavered where I stood.

The gentle breeze floated up to me from the lake far below and whisked around me, cold and comforting. That monster I killed was only the start of this war. There would be no round three, no third battle for another group of heirs. The wind breathed this along my skin like a confirmation that said all was lost if I gave up here. I was allowed to be angry. I wasn't allowed to quit.

"Sox...?" Gawain said my name again. "I'm sorry."

CHAPTER TWELVE

Mirror Sickness

My head was foggy as I descended from the castle ruins. The pebbles crunched beneath my riding boots. They were well worn and the most comfortable pair of shoes I had ever owned. I trained with my sword in these boots. I danced in these boots, though my instructor hated it. The leather was supple and I cleaned and oiled them religiously.

Velvety laughter tore me away from my empty thoughts as I stepped from the rough path and into the grass of the valley. The afternoon sun was warm, almost hot and little bugs chittered by my ears. They were so loud they almost sounded like human voices and I swatted at them to stop.

The pain of my injuries had come and gone. At first it was agony and then nothing. I had avoided examining the wounds. The blood had stopped running, clotted by the fabric of my green shirt. I was sticky. I reeked with that awful metallic scent. I liked this shirt... It was an olive green long-sleeve top made of soft fabric that was still somehow thick enough that I didn't need an undershirt. It was the most adult shirt I had, and that thing had ruined it.

This way! A voice giggled within my mind, overwhelming my sense of self and that voice that I had come to recognize as Galahad's. I heaved a sigh. She was teasing me, there for a moment and gone the second I thought I had found where she was coming from. I had left the castle ruins to find her. She resonated within me like a wind chime on a perfect day.

This way! She called to me again. Was I not going fast enough? I didn't have a horse and there weren't roads down to the valley anymore. The path was steep and rocky and slow.

Sweat beaded along my skin and I reached back to wipe my neck with my palm. It dripped down along my sides, soaking the parts of my shirt that weren't already sticky with drying blood. As it soaked into my wounds, they stung and my nose wrinkled at the irritation. I needed to head back to the village and find someone to look at this. That creature wasn't real, or it was something made of magic. There was no telling what its bite would do to me.

I took my next steps down toward the village. The heat and the sweat was making me thirsty. I didn't know of any water nearby. The stream I had jumped on horseback was high on the hill beneath the broken bridge. I wasn't going to travel all the way back up just for a drink and then hike all the way back down. There had to be something between me and the village. I was too thirsty to make it to the lake. Not that I wanted to drink that grimy fish water anyway.

The gentle babble moving water caught my ears and I turned. Right beside me, flowing from further up the valley and into the hills was a noisy little brook.

How convenient! And how silly of me to have not seen it before.

I stiffly knelt down at the water's edge and plunged my hands into it. The water was warm and no matter how much I drank, it didn't seem to help much. I was dehydrated and exhausted. Certainly that was the issue. This had been a long day, and the one before it had been longer.

I breathed heavily, my lungs desperate for air and I splashed water across my face to cool off. As the stream steadied from my intrusion and I caught a glimpse of my reflection, I frowned. My face was there. I was there. I stared into the water and when my eyes met my own, I realized the face looking back at me wasn't mine at all. The world around me slid away and I found myself kneeling before Murphy. The grass beneath me was soft and green in a field that seemed to stretch on and on forever parallel to a silky sky illuminated in violets and pinks.

"I wasn't expecting *you*," he said and his voice echoed in my head as if he spoke through a toilet paper tube at the far end of a tunnel. He bent, a hand on his knee and his other outstretched toward me. "The Questing Beast was supposed to be for the heir of Perceval. You are not the heir of Perceval."

My head felt hazy and my body felt disjointed like I floated around inside myself.

"What do you want with Sir Perceval?" I wouldn't give him her name. If he didn't know it, I wouldn't enlighten him.

"Well," Murphy said and crouched down before me as if he were meeting level of a child. "Perceval was the original grail knight, so, I guess it has something to do with that. No heir of Bors, and my lady Morgan le Fay didn't think you were capable of being swayed. So count me absolutely flabbergasted."

I had only ever read that word: flabbergasted. It sounded weird. Like shenanigans. Or gobbledygook. I was thinking in gobbledygook. My brain was mush and I couldn't keep my thoughts together. I blinked. I shut my eyes tight and rubbed them roughly before I opened them again.

"The heir of Perceval wouldn't be swayed by the likes of you," I said. The world swam around me and for a second. I pitched to the side, unbalanced and braced myself with my hand planted against the ground. My head went back. I looked up at the sky.

I could hear the bugs chittering again, murmuring little things to one another. They weren't quite so loud here.

"Easy there," Murphy chuckled. His hand swept behind my head and gently brought my attention back to him.

"What is this?" I asked. I felt weak and my voice reflected it. "Where am I?"

"Playing with your reflection in a stream that doesn't exist," he said. "You're lucky the questing beast wasn't real, or you'd most certainly be dead."

He smiled to me reassuringly and I wanted to hit him. I wanted to knock that smile entirely off his face. I wanted to hit him so hard that his head rolled down his esophagus and shot out of his ass.

"I don't know what that look is," he said to me, his smile faltering. "But I can see the violence in your eyes. You might be the heir of Galahad, but you are no knight of Camelot."

"You're right," I said, my head slowly nodding. "Remind me to kill you when I get a chance."

He smiled broadly. "Kill a questing beast and think you can take on the rest of us awful, wicked things?"

"Nah, just you," I said. My teeth grit together as I fought to keep myself upright. My energy waned as if the life were being sucked right out of me. My hands felt heavy. My shoulders drooped.

"And if I beg for mercy?" he asked. He knew of the oaths Merlin asked us to take. Had Mordred been a knight?

"I'll make you beg for mercy," I said, swallowing dryly. "And then I'll turn the volume up on my favorite song." I didn't know if that was an empty threat. Something stirred within me as I spoke and I leaned into it, into the strength that helped me feel a little more stable. I grasped tightly to that crutch, dug into it to stay upright and conscious.

Murphy's smile faltered as he brushed his fingers over my hair. "This is a wicked curse, Galahad," he told me. "You're better off not fighting this. The creature that bit you left a mark. If we do not find you, you will find us. You'll search for me in your reflection, and when I do not come for you, you'll keep searching. You'll go through anyone or anything in your way. The battle is coming, Galahad. And you have been chosen for our side."

"Like the last person picked at kickball," I scoffed.

He continued on like he hadn't heard me. It wasn't an endearing trait.

"I'm glad it's you though," he said with that all too genuine smile. "I already know you, and our ancestors were quite good friends. I'd like to get to know you better."

"The only way you can make friends is by taking away their free will?" I asked and barely managed a smile. My breath shuddered in my lungs as I struggled to keep breathing. "Aren't you a peach…"

Murphy sighed heavily and dryly huffed, "As much of a peach as you are, my dear."

I struck his hand, knocked it away from me. The world shattered and fractured around me and fell away like glitter. There was no stream. There was no water. There was no… anything. I knelt in darkness, able to see myself and nothing else.

My body ached. I felt the injuries from the beast and

186

groaned as I tried to push myself to my feet. I staggered and fell to my side. Everything felt weak. I needed help. I didn't know where I was. I had to get out of here. I had to find Merlin.

I should have told him when all of this started. I should have mentioned the first time I had visions. My mother had told me to trust Merlin and I hadn't.

I was scared.

Do not run away.

I couldn't move, even if I wanted to.

The world didn't make much sense. It blurred in and out. I was jostled on the back of a horse as someone's arms held me tightly while the animal beneath us raced at a breakneck pace. I felt the soft, steadiness of my bed. Merlin's bright blue eyes stared back at me and I saw his old and bearded face superimposed with a much younger version with dark hair. The eyes were the same. The younger Merlin... he was handsome.

"Socorro?" he said and I saw the old sorcerer a little clearer. He set a wet cloth on my forehead. "You need to rest."

"Reflections!" The word shot past my lips in delirium.

"Look at her eyes," someone whispered. I didn't recognize their voice.

"No!" I screamed. "No reflections. No reflections." I covered my eyes with my hands and when someone grabbed my wrists, I lashed out and struggled for freedom.

"Stop," Merlin ordered and I wasn't certain if the order was for me or for them. I was released and felt a tug on my shirt along my wounded side. I swiped the hand that touched me.

"Your wound," Merlin said. "I need to see it."

Gently my shirt rose with the sound of wet paper tearing. I

felt the tug at the injuries and gasped as each one was reopened. Blood ran anew. I was getting blood on my bed.

Murmurs filled the room and I opened a bleary eye to look about at their blurry shapes. Not a single one of them other than Merlin appeared whole and clear. Who were these shapeless and ghostly shadows around my room?

The warlock touched my side below my ribs, tracing a shape. "Socorro..." he said softly and I looked. I shouldn't have looked.

Tears streamed silently from my eyes. Murphy was right, I was marked. On my side was the rampant black lion, the symbol of Morgan le Fay. Her father Gorlois had been three red lion heads roaring in a field of black. She had taken her own symbol from that. The lion was strong; the black lion was dangerous. And this lion was inset into my skin like a burn. A brand.

"Marked..." I muttered over and over again, unable to control that word and keep it from tumbling endlessly out of my mouth. I wanted to stop it but my brain wasn't working. I had no control over myself.

"What's wrong with her?" came another voice. It sounded familiar and so far away. I didn't know who was speaking. I looked around wildly at them, my eyes wide and my fear seeping through every pore. One of the shadows stared back at me in my insanity. Were the shadows real people? Was this another trick?

"Reflections..." Merlin muttered softly to himself. He shook his head and I focused on the long white strands of his beard as they swayed with the movement. "I believe she suffers from mirror sickness."

If Merlin replied, then the speaker was real. The shadow was a person. The shadows were people. I tried to remember that, though the thought was slipping away the moment I managed to manifest it. I repeated it endlessly. "The shadows are people. The shadows are people."

"What the hell is mirror sickness?" someone shouted. I could hear the panic in his voice. What person would be worried about me? Gawain was right. I wasn't good enough to help him and I had become more trouble than I was worth.

I looked up and Merlin held out a glass of water. "You need to drink," he said. "Your fever is getting worse."

I saw it. My face shone in the crystal. Since when did we have drinking glasses? It was goblets and mugs of wood and hard metal, or plastic cups that some of the heirs had sneaked in when they thought no one was looking. Eddel didn't have glass cups.

The face in the crystal was my own for only a second. And then Murphy's knowing smile replaced my reflection. I blinked and was back in that place, sitting beside him in the green grass with the soft purple sky overhead full of pink clouds.

"Looking for me already?" he asked as he leaned toward me and bumped me with his shoulder.

"No," I replied shortly. My mind was steadier here even if my body still felt disjointed. I could think here even if I couldn't move very well. "What's wrong with me?"

"That..." he said slowly, "I feel that is a loaded question." He looked at me skeptically and added, "I suppose I could give you an answer but I feel like this is a trap."

"This!" I shouted and gestured around me. "This is a trap, Murphy! Let me go!"

My arm stayed lifted, floating in front of me. I hadn't been able to lower it.

"I can't," he told me as he reached out to gently touch my wrist and bring my hand back to my lap. "It isn't up to me."

"How do I get rid of that mark?" I couldn't keep the fear out of my voice. "You burned it into me."

"I did nothing of the sort." He shook his head and sighed, "Accept it, Galahad. Come to us and after we've obtained the grail, I'm certain you can go free."

"You don't call the shots. She does."

"That's true. I can't promise you anything other than what I can do myself," he said.

"And what is it that you can do?"

He smiled. "Nothing."

"Then you're just as useless as I am," I spat back at him.

"No, Galahad," he said softly. His brows furrowed and he shook his head. "No, you're the most useful person in the world right now."

He drew up his knees and rest his arms atop them as he stared out at something beyond the hazy blue horizon. "Whoever told you that you were useless is wrong," he said, his voice low.

Murphy sounded irritated, but not at me.

I blinked slowly and felt heavy again. My strength wavered. I'd managed myself well on this second visit but I didn't know how much longer I could keep it up. How many more times would I be sucked into this world?

"Galahad," he began slowly and brought his gaze back to me. I managed to meet his eyes but my head was hard to hold up. "The longer you fight the mirror sickness, the weaker you'll become. You're losing your mind out there. Please... just one step in the right direction and your path will be clearer."

I couldn't be sure of the expression on my face, though I

knew in my heart I couldn't trust him. He was the serpent's head of the questing beast. A snake, I could trust. This man before me, I could not. Or, perhaps, I could trust that I could not trust him. Even if he sounded like he was pleading for my sake.

"I'm done here," I declared and the space between us fractured like broken glass. The crackling etched and scratched downward until he fell to pieces before me. I looked down at myself, expecting my own image to break. I remained whole as I patted my body all over for certainty. Would I burst in this madness as well? Would I shatter the moment I raised my voice?

Merlin sat on the side of my bed with a wooden mug extended toward me. There had been no glass at all. I was seeking a reflection and my mind had tricked me. In anger, I struck it from his hand and sent it flying across the room. Shadowy spectators gasped and shuffled where they stood.

"Please leave us," Merlin told them and they hesitated before filing out of the room.

"Socorro," Merlin said to me, his voice soft and careful. "You're sick."

"Make me better!" I shouted in his face.

"I cannot," he said. "Magic is tricky and attempting to heal you could kill you. You know this."

I did know that. Magic wasn't something that could solve all of life's problems. This was something Merlin had drilled into my head during our lessons. Strong magic fighting strong magic within an individual could kill it. My body couldn't handle the internal war of Merlin and Morgan le Fay.

"Then leave," I growled. The word echoed off my tongue. It echoed in my head. It filled every open space in my room and I shrieked as the sound grew louder. I covered my ears and sank to my bed thrashing and wailing.

Silence.

I didn't know how long I screamed at nothing and everything all at once. In a moment of clarity, I sat up and the world wavered around me as if I were in some kind of dream. I looked at my hands and they were defined and sharp. I was whole. There was no one in my room and the shadows were gone. But so had Merlin. They had left me.

Lifting my shirt, I looked down at the wounds on my body. They were wrapped in gauze and I tore the bandages and flung them aside. The teeth of the Questing Beast had left inch long marks across my stomach in an arch that nearly reached my right side. The scabs were rough and a few began to bleed again. I had reopened them by ripping away their coverings.

Along my left side was the black lion, standing on its back feet as if rearing in battle, or defiance. My first tattoo. I chuckled.

This wasn't funny. I shook my head.

I turned and draped my legs off the side of my bed. My feet touched to the cold wooden floor and it felt like a shot of electricity through my entire nervous system. I shuddered. I needed socks. Ha. Sox.

Brain was muddy. I rose to my feet and careened sideways into the wall. My shoulder slammed against it and I grunted.

My socks were in the bottom drawer of my dresser. I doubted I would be able to bend down and reach them without falling onto the floor, or through the floor. What world lay beyond the floor?

I slid my bare feet across the wooden floor, my arms out at my side for balance. I slapped my hand on top of the dresser and held tightly to it to stop the world from spinning around me and throwing me into the abyss.

My rolled pair of socks sat on top of the dresser where I had left it over a month ago when Gawain returned them to me. I stared at them. They still smelled like the lake. They were discolored and I could see them crystal clear.

I needed sock to go anywhere. I needed them. My fingers were incapable of simply picking them up and I slapped my hand on them and dragged them toward me. There was a folded note beside where the socks had been. I couldn't remember who had written it.

Socks in one hand, I leaned forward against the drawers to free up my other hand and I opened the note to read it. The letters were blurry. I squinted to see what was written. Three words. I turned my head left, but it didn't make it any clearer. I tilted my head all the way to the right and there was still no success. My head began to hurt. Closing my eyes, I thought to cast the note away. It couldn't be that important, could it? If I hadn't read it before, why did I need to read it at that exact moment?

Deep breath in, deep breath out. I stared at the piece of soft paper and tried again. The words hurt my eyes, but still, I kept trying. Who had written it? And why had I kept it and never read it?

"Let me read it," I growled at the wobbling world.

The words snapped into focus: *Soul - Matchbox Twenty*.

Gawain.

This was my song.

I couldn't recall the lyrics. I had listened to it on his playlist. I was sure it was on my phone, too. Especially after I had updated my music at my mom's house. A lot of his songs had migrated over to my collection.

My peripheral vision was hazy, but everything immediately in front of me was clear. Yelling at the spell had forced it back. Unknowingly I had fought it and gained space. I still felt enclosed, stuffed in a box somewhere in the back of a closet.

I dropped the note back where it had sat for weeks and stumbled over my own feet to sit on my bed. Socks. I had my socks and I put them on my feet. The world felt infinitely warmer. Shoes would help. I gazed languidly around and found them sitting beside the door next to my sword. Wouldn't I need that as well?

My assumption about reaching down for the sock drawer was correct. When I went for my boots, I pitched forward and struck my head on the wall. I keeled over onto my side but that didn't stop me from pulling on my shoes. Right shoe. Left shoe. I squirmed awkwardly on the floor as I tightened my sword belt around my waist.

Flat on my back, I gazed up at the ceiling of my room. I had never looked before at the old wooden rafters. I deserved better than a thatch roof. Didn't I?

Haphazardly flinging myself to my feet, I wobbled unsteadily and fell forward against the closed door, shoving it open. I spilled out into the next room where shadows stared back at me from the table.

"Shadows," I breathed, and I felt the saliva spill from my mouth like a rabid animal.

"Get Merlin," one of them said and another ran out the front door. Three were left. Three tall, shapeless blobs of undulating black, tar-like flesh and glowing yellow eyes. They weren't airy ghosts anymore.

Sunlight of the late afternoon flickered off of a sword across the room. Had I been in better health, I knew I could not see my reflection from where I stood. My mind reached for the possibility. I yearned for it. I could see my face, could see Murphy waiting patiently in that field of green for me to come back to him.

"No," I whispered. I tried to fight it, tried to pull away. There was nothing I could have done that would have kept me from going back to him.

Murphy sat upon a large stone that hadn't been there before. He smiled up at me and scooted over a little to make space. "Sit with me," he said and patted the rock beside him.

My body swayed forward, determined to listen to him. I had no more control of myself here than I did outside and my mind was fading just as fast. "Come Sit With Me," I muttered, fighting for some sense of self. "Laura... Souguellis."

Sitting with Murphy was too comfortable. I had fought him the first time, refused to say who Sir Perceval was, but if he wanted that information or information about anything else, I couldn't trust what I might say in my growing delirium.

His brows raised and he held out his hand. "Galahad."

If I could avoid speaking to him, I could keep my mind. The way he spoke to me was like a siren song and I if I kept him at a distance I wouldn't succumb to the spell. But the song I had said played around me and was no different than if he pulled me in by my hand. I wanted to go to him. I wanted to rip my feet from the ground and float to him.

"You can see the castle from here," he said.

Castle. What castle? Surely not Camelot. I turned my head to look. There was nothing there but the endless plain of green grass and deepening purple sky. The pink clouds felt sickly and looking at them made me nauseous.

"You can't see it unless you take my hand," he said.

"Take My Hand," I muttered. "The Cab."

I was playing Gawain's game wrong. No. Gawain's game was right. Use the song to summarize a situation. I was trying to avoid speaking, but I could see myself running away if I put my hand in his.

I had to play the game differently. Reverse it. Use a song that meant the opposite. But there was a castle out there somewhere that I was unable to see. I wanted to see it. I liked castles, even when they were just giant piles of pretty rocks.

Murphy wasn't the enemy, he was trying to help me see the castle. If I went with him, the agony of this mirror sickness would be over. There were so many things I could do if I weren't sick. Like see a castle.

I wanted it to be over. None of the thoughts coursing through my brain meat made sense anymore.

Murphy tilted his head. "Are you coming?" he asked.

"Not Afraid," I said. "Earshot."

"Are those song titles?" he asked as he slid down from the rock and stepped toward me. "I'm sorry, I don't understand what it is you're trying to say."

Good, he didn't understand me. Bad, he was closing the distance between us. I had to think clearly. I had to focus. Both of those things were difficult when I couldn't trust the struggle in my mind. I shut my eyes and clenched my fists.

I needed to remember that he was the enemy. It was hard to hate him.

"Galahad?" he asked.

I couldn't trust my feelings. I didn't want to hate him. I wanted to trust him. I wanted to run away to him. No, I wanted to stay in the sanctuary.

"You should go back now," he said comfortingly. "You have a bit of a journey ahead of you to get to my side. You shouldn't wear yourself out here."

Murphy sighed heavily and his cold fingertips gently brushed my cheek. I wasn't used to touch like this. It felt... right.

"You're not well..." he said. "I'll have a warm bed waiting for when you arrive. And more food than you know what to do with. Good food."

I kept my eyes closed. What would happen if I went back to where all of those creatures were? I didn't want to go without him.

"It's going to be okay, Galahad," he assured me. "Ease your mind, and come home."

Once more he shattered. I heard it and I looked to see him break into thousands of glittering pieces once again.

I staggered back and slumped against the door frame of my room.

"Socorro?" a shadow asked, carefully crossing the wooden floor to touch my shoulder.

I drew my sword with a wild swing and the shadow leapt away. "Are you crazy?" it shouted.

Possible. It was entirely possible I had long ago lost my mind. I couldn't discern who these shadows were supposed to be though I could swear I knew the voices. I should have been able to make an assumption, to put the two together and know that I was among friends. The moment that thought crossed my mind it was as if the voices became even stranger. They overlapped as if a multitude of people spoke at the same time. They were male and female, creature and human. Real... not real?

I needed another reflection. I needed Murphy. I was starved for the face that looked back at me, that offered me a hand and kind words. I was yearned to have my mind make sense again.

I had to find Murphy.

"Look at her eyes," a shadow whispered.

They stared at me. As I watched them, I wondered how I looked: completely unable to control my own body, lost to someone else's control of my consciousness.

I was compelled to move. The tip of my sword dragged along the floor as I crossed the threshold with trudging steps. The desire for a reflection overwhelmed me. I needed a mirror, and there were none in this place. The village had no mirrors. The heirs were not to be vain.

Vanity was not what I sought. I sought him. My reflection was the key to finding Murphy and I needed him like I needed air.

I staggered forward, the shadows quietly trailing behind. They didn't engage. That was fine. I didn't mind them as long as they didn't intervene.

Moving through the hazy village, shadows stood along the path ahead. They watched me with wide, glowing yellow eyes as I drooled and stumbled forward in my rabid state. They could stare. I didn't need them. If I reached the white arches, I could summon a portal. I could find a place with a mirror, a solid mirror instead of some trick of my mind.

A shadow stepped into my path, a big one. "Where are you going, Ilar?" it demanded.

Only one person called me Ilar. I didn't know who that was. I tilted my head and my face scrunched as I tried to think past the want in my soul. This was someone I knew.

"Go back to bed," it told me.

My head tilted back. If the sun shined on something, surely that shining thing was a reflection. I tilted my head the other way, scanning for anything the light touched. There had to be something. I rolled my neck, longing for anything.

My sword! Swords were metal. Metal reflected light. I held it up to catch the sun. No matter which direction I turned it, there was nothing here. Cheap reflections wouldn't help me anymore. I had to keep going.

"Ilar!" the shadow shouted.

What did it want? This creature was in my way. If it didn't move, I would make it move.

It took a step toward me. I matched its movement. If it continued to advance, I would not stand down. I would not be stopped from reaching my goal.

My goal. Yes. Murphy was my goal. I had to keep moving. I had to see him.

I tried to speak. Words failed me and my mouth moved like someone had muted the television. No more rambling, no more repetitive words. I didn't need words. They were useless.

"Ilar..." it said slowly. "Socorro," it corrected. "You're not well."

Its next step was tentative, but it was still a step. I leapt at it. The shadow crossed a blade in front of its chest and mine struck with a resounding clang of metal. It brushed it away as if I hadn't the strength to hold it back. It was a large shadow. Had I been in my right mind I would have known without a doubt I was no match. I did not know this anymore.

"What are you doing?" it shouted.

The murmuring of the black shapes around us grew louder and more concerned.

His stance was similar to mine. We both stood with weapons lowered, relaxed and ready.

I swung again. I brought my sword around in a wide arc

that my enemy would see coming. This shadow was fond of me and I could use it to my advantage. It knocked my sword away and I spun with it, ducking under the shadow's arm as I came around and swept its right leg out from under its body with my foot. It fell to its knee. Shadows still had knees. As its sword came up, mine came down, and I struck the shadow across the face with the pommel.

The shadow fell. It didn't move.

It shouldn't have stood in my way.

I turned again to leave and my path was blocked. "No!" someone called out, though I couldn't tell who. The shadows were blending together as a singular mass, as a wall. "Let her pass. Let her go."

They parted and I didn't wait for permission. I kept walking. My sword kept dragging. The sound of my boots tapped up the stairs and the edge of my blade matched the sound as it clanked behind me. What did I care? This sword wasn't mine, it was a practice foil. Garbage. They never gave me one of my own. I hadn't earned it yet. That was fine, I didn't want it anyway. I didn't want to fight for them anymore.

CHAPTER THIRTEEN

Morgan le Fay

When I reached the archways, I squinted my eyes and stared at them. Did they all lead to everywhere? I wasn't certain. They were dizzying, disorienting and blurring together the more I looked at them. Shouldn't they take me where I wanted to go? Why would they prevent me from traveling through them?

Did I know where I wanted to go? Yes, the place with the purple sky. That's where Murphy was. That was where I needed to go and I put my hands on a pillar and demanded to be taken to him.

A portal opened within the archway and the world on the other side was much darker than where I stood. Even with the light of burning torches casting orange circles on the rocky ground, visibility only went so far.

Was Murphy in a cave? For what reason? Where was the grass plain? Where was that castle he wanted me to see?

I confidently strode through the portal to the other side and the air rushed from my lungs. My sight darkened and I collapsed to my knees. I struck the sword in the ground in an effort to keep myself upright and pressed my forehead against the hilt as my weight sagged against the shining steel. It reflected the light once again. The spell had eaten away at my mind.

My chest heaved and my body trembled, aching with the pain of the questing beast's bite and the exhaustion of fighting the fever that had consumed me. My face felt wet. I wiped at my mouth with my shirtsleeve. I wiped away the mad drool that ran down my neck and soaked into my shirt. Pain rippled through my head. I shut my eyes tightly. Everything hurt.

"Socorro?" I heard. Eddel. It was Eddel. I would know her voice anywhere. I wanted to get up, to grab her and hold tight. I couldn't move.

"Eddel...?" was my exhausted reply, more air than speech.

"You know me now?" She came around to kneel in front of me, her shadow fell over my sword and her cautious hand settled on my wrist.

"Yeah, I know you," I said, swallowing hard at the dry lump in my throat. The brook had never existed.

"Oh thank God," she cried and leaned into me, her forehead upon my shoulder. Her hand balled into my shirt, though she didn't pull me any closer as I rest against my sword. "Socorro, Gawain and Henry are here too," she said. "What is going on?"

I didn't know if I had the strength to speak and hold myself up at the same time and I slowly let myself sink to my knees. I slid out of Eddel's grasp and she reached out and took my hand in hers. I was exhausted, but that little comfort gave me the ability to push through. I told them what I knew, that the questing beast was meant for the heir of Perceval. That Murphy, the heir of Mordred, was looking for a grail knight. I told them about the mirror sickness Merlin told me I had and the visions of Murphy, how I had to find him. I needed to find him. I told them everything my brain knew and thought it knew and watched their faces fill with horror.

My mind was better here, I could see even though my eyes ached in the dark. My throat was parched. I still felt that longing to see Murphy again, but I could think my own thoughts. Best of all, I knew who my friends were.

"Where are we, exactly?" Henry asked.

Groaning, I rose to my feet and took the time to put my sword back into the sheath at my left hip. "Somewhere on the path to Murphy," I said slowly.

"Can we turn back?" Gawain asked.

I glanced at him over my shoulder and said, "You can."

His dark brows furrowed, casting an even darker shadow over his face. "That's not what I meant and you know it."

"I'm not stupid," I told him. "I know what you meant."

"What has gotten into you two?" Eddel hissed. "We don't have time for your bickering. We have to figure this... Socorro?"

I stared unblinkingly down the path ahead of us. "I'm sorry. I have to go," I sighed and shuffled forward.

"Socorro!" Henry called out, "Wait!" He rushed to my side and his hand touched my shoulder.

"Wait...?" I muttered. "Wait for what?"

"What are you going to do when you get there?" Henry asked. "What's at the end of the hall? What are you trying to accomplish?"

"I don't have a choice," I said. Had they not been listening to me? Did they think I was joking? "If I go back, I'll be a drooling heap searching for reflections in tree bark while I can't recognize anyone around me. And if I go forward, well, maybe I'll be useful."

"Sox," Gawain grumbled. "Don't be like that."

"I'd say you're already useful," Henry said with a broad grin. "You knocked your father unconscious with some dirty sword work."

"Was that who the shadow was?" Of course. My father was the only one who called me Ilar. The sickness had kept that recognition from me. "If I go back to the village I put all of you at risk," I said as I put one foot in front of the other. I didn't mean to. I didn't realize I was moving again until I reached the bend in the path.

Eddel rushed ahead of me, blocking my way. "We can figure it out!" she pleaded.

I looked back into her dark eyes and smiled tiredly. The village, the rest of the heirs. They would all be lost if Morgan le Fay ensnared her. "The questing beast was meant for you, Eddel," I said. "It almost got Gawain. I've only been in the village for a few months. I have the least amount of secrets to spill."

Her expression fell. What had I done in my life to ever deserve friends like these. They cared about me, even if they couldn't save me.

Eddel withdrew and my steps resumed.

"Socorro," Henry shot out in front of me. My hand dropped to the hilt of my sword and he reached forward and placed his hands on mine, keeping me from drawing. "Easy there," he said. "You see me, right? It's Henry. Not a shadow."

Not a shadow. I knew Henry. I had to remind myself when I never had to before.

"You can't control this can you?" he asked softly. His hands squeezed mine.

"No," I said as my bravado shook. Words were failing me again. I was taking too long. Henry delayed me and I wanted nothing more than to shove him aside and run. For the moment, I still had my mind. I struggled to keep it.

"What are we supposed to do?" he asked.

Henry didn't want to fail me, even though he owed me nothing.

"I dunno, Henry," I said, "I don't envy your position in all this."

He bit back a smirk. "Is that so...?" He slowly removed his hands from mine.

I continued, "Without me in the village, Morgan le Fay won't be able to find you again, I think.

Henry's eyes glistened. He blinked and it was gone. "We won't be whole without you."

"Maybe this is a good thing, Henry. It buys everyone some time," I told him. "And if I can throw a wrench in their plans, we all know I will."

"Find a good wrench," Henry said as he stepped back.

With my path no longer blocked, desperation surged within me. I had to hold it back, that longing that wasn't mine. It sickened me how my heart wished to run away, how my mind demanded I find Murphy.

I put one foot in front of another and silence followed me down the stone corridor. The light grew brighter and the surging sound of water steadily grew louder.

"I wish it was me," Eddel whispered and her voice carried in the cavern.

"Don't wish that," I said. "You're one of our leaders. If we lost you, Henry would be on his own. Stay safe for Henry's sake. He's a terrible leader."

"Socorro!" Henry balked and the other two chuckled.

The cave fell away. We stepped out onto a long ledge where water blocked the path ahead. It wasn't a little stream of water, but a massive fall. The water coursed from above in nearly neon blue. It reminded me of the colored water at a putt-putt mini golf course.

The surging falls swept aside, opening like a curtain. Murphy stood, revealed to us like an actor on stage.

Two quick steps forward and I slid to a halt. I ground my heels into the stone and held fast. I didn't want to go, but my heart belonged to him.

"You finally came," he said with a lopsided smile. "Galahad, you didn't have to bring your friends."

Swords drew behind me.

"Oh come now," Murphy sighed. "They weren't invited."

"Where is she?" I demanded. "The one you serve."

"Why would she be here? Am I not enough for you?" he asked. He looked genuinely offended.

"No."

He touched his hand to his heart. "Galahad, you wound me."

"Is it fatal?" I spat.

"I'm glad you're no longer spouting song titles at me," he said with a polite smile. "We don't have the same taste in music."

"Oh good," I grumbled. "I'd hate that."

Murphy once again held out his hand to me. "Time to go Galahad."

"No." I shook my head.

"You'll meet our lady in due time."

"That due time is now," I said and crossed my arms. I could hold it. I could see him and I had the patience to wait him out. I didn't want to go after all, but if I absolutely had to, then I wanted to see her first. I had to know that she was real. My friends had to tell Merlin that Morgan le Fay had returned.

Murphy's amusement faltered. His jaw clenched. I wasn't playing his game. He didn't seem to have the time that I did.

Enough.

The word echoed through my mind with such force that my bones rattled.

She stood beside him, appearing from nothing and only taller than me because of the heels on her boots. She was dressed like anyone with a little bit of money and an actual sense of style. Black leggings, knee high boots, and a layering of red and black shirts because women's clothes were made too thin. She had been in the outside world and didn't seem to like it.

"Are you sated, Galahad?" she asked me. Her voice was the one that laughed in Camelot. That melodious sound that mocked my injury by the questing beast. She had demanded I find her and I finally had.

"Morgan le Fay," Henry whispered.

"And who do you belong to?" she asked him with a sly smile on her red lips.

Henry quieted. We all did. If she didn't know, we wouldn't tell her. But, then how had Murphy known who I was at the movie theater?

I didn't want to think of it. It was worth some thought, but my head was feeling fuzzy in her presence.

"Sure," I replied to her and stepped forward.

A hand gripped my wrist and whipped me around. Gawain stood smaller than he had before. The cave was dark and he was no longer radiant the way he had appeared to me in the light of the ruins of Camelot.

"Don't go," he pleaded. "Fight this. Come home." He shook his head and his mop of hair shook back and forth.

"I'm sorry. About what I said in Camelot. I'm so sorry."

"Gawain," I said and his green eyes shot up to my face. "Move."

He took a sharp breath, a gasp, as if my words had struck him somewhere deep inside. The way his words had done to me.

I reached deep into my pocket and offered him my phone. "Audio Adrenaline."

"Sox..." he whimpered.

"Pin is one-four-one-five," I told him.

"Of course it is," he said as he took it from me, clutching it in his fingers. He didn't release me.

Henry and Eddel stood there with their swords lowered. They had drawn like Gawain at the sight of Murphy and we all stared at one another as if this were our final farewell. I wanted to guarantee that we would see each other again, but we all knew we were the last descendants of the Knights of the Round Table. Anything could happen, and there would be no more of us to fight for Camelot, for the world.

I tried my best to give them a reassuring smile and then I took a deep breath and gave in to the pull of the mirror sickness. My feet led me away from my fellow heirs. My arm stretched back behind me and I gave them one last glance before Gawain finally let me go.

Morgan le Fay was beautiful. Her dark hair fell in long waving layers along her shoulders and down her back.

When I was clear of the waterfall, it fell into place behind me like a curtain drawing shut at the end of a play. I felt the air it shoved aside. The water misted over my shoulders. My face felt cold.

"Pleasure to meet you Galahad," she said.

"There is no pleasure in this," I replied.

She dismissed my words with a wave of her hand. "Details."

"You can't force my obedience," I said defiantly.

She raised her hand and a worn and beaten metal cup appeared. "Then you'll drink this," she said.

"My Lady…" Murphy softly objected.

"I'm not drinking a damn thing."

The world quaked around me and I heard the others cry out on the other side of the waterfall. I turned to go after them. Hitting the water was like hitting a wall and it knocked me off of my feet and flattened me against the rock. I crawled out, soaked through.

"If you do not drink, then I cannot guarantee the safety of your friends," she nearly sang.

Murphy looked away.

I rushed her and snatched the cup out of her hand. I glared at her. I let her see that just because I drank from that cup, it would not be the end of this. It didn't matter if I made this sacrifice. I would not bow to her. I wouldn't find this grail for her. I didn't even want to find it for Merlin.

I touched the cup to my lips and upended it. The liquid was sweet as it slid across my tongue; it was cold as it filled my stomach. I tossed the cup away and it clattered on the stone before falling off the side of the walkway and disappearing down into the deep unending dark below.

"Hey Morgan le Fay," I said sweetly as my vision began to blur, as sounds became white noise and the memory of the village faded from my mind. "Get fucked."

www.ingramcontent.com/pod-product-compliance
Lightning Source LLC
Chambersburg PA
CBHW022059170626
46808CB00002B/506